"You

Diego's heart plummeted as he realized Kate's mistake.

"I'm not Jose," he fina

The smile dropped fr
shocked as he felt. "D

Diego nodded. She c
hands. "Oh, my God, y

"I'm so sorry," he blurted out in a rush. "I thought this room was empty and—"

And never expected to find myself kissing the woman of my dreams, he finished in his thoughts.

Kate shook her head, still not looking at him. "It's not your fault. I just assumed..."

"I'm going to go," he mumbled, not sure what else there was to say.

His attraction to Kate before was nothing compared to his feelings now that he'd kissed her, held her in his arms, and he let out a deep sigh.

He was sure it had been an innocent mistake, but her innocent mistake had just stuck him into a whole heap of trouble.

Dear Reader,

This book was a joy to write, even if it sometimes felt like a juggling act to get time to work with both a toddler and a newborn in my life. Time to write occasionally felt like a punishment when all I wanted was sleep, but often it felt like a safe haven away from the chaos that is little kids. Even when it was difficult to find the chance to get words on the page, though, I knew Diego's story needed to be told, and I was so excited to watch it unfold.

What surprised me, though, was how much I came to like Jose as I wrote. In some ways he's a difficult person to love, but he's also wonderful in his own way. I would love to be the jokester in people's lives, and I don't think I'm alone in that wish. So I was looking forward to his story as much as I was Diego's.

The McNeals are a caring, loving family, and I've enjoyed writing about them. I'm sorry to say goodbye to them, but I'm so happy that they all got their happy endings before I did. I hope their stories speak to you and remind you what's really important in life.

Happy reading!

Ali

HOME *on the* RANCH

HONORABLE TEXAS COWBOY

ALI OLSON

HARLEQUIN® HOME ON THE RANCH

ISBN-13: 978-1-335-00561-8
ISBN-13: 978-1-335-63396-5 (Direct to Consumer edition)

Home on the Ranch: Honorable Texas Cowboy

This edition published by arrangement with Harlequin Books S.A.

For questions and comments about the quality of this book, please contact us at CustomerService@Harlequin.com.

HARLEQUIN®
www.Harlequin.com

Printed in U.S.A.

Ali Olson is a longtime resident of Las Vegas, Nevada, where she has been teaching English at the high school and college level for the past seven years. Ali has found a passion for writing sexy romance novels, both contemporary and historical, and is enthusiastic about her newly discovered career. She loves reading, writing and traveling with her husband and constant companion, Joe. She appreciates hearing from readers. Write to her at authoraliolson.com.

Books by Ali Olson

Harlequin Western Romance

Spring Valley, Texas

The Bull Rider's Twin Trouble
The Cowboy's Surprise Baby

Harlequin Blaze

Her Sexy Vegas Cowboy
Her Sexy Texas Cowboy

Visit the Author Profile page
at Harlequin.com for more titles.

For little Cassian.
I'm grateful every day to have you in my life.
Thank you for every smile, every kiss and every laugh
you've given me since you came into this world.

Chapter 1

Diego McNeal's headlights washed over the old farmhouse where he'd grown up, bathing it in bright light for a few seconds before he turned off the engine and everything faded into darkness. Everything but the small light over the door, which Ma had left on for him, as she always did for her children when they would be coming home late.

And boy, was it late. Diego's eyes stung. He stretched his back and rolled his neck, trying to rid himself of the perpetual ache that had lodged there over the past few months. Even though he was only twenty-seven, sitting at a desk and dealing with the stress of running a business made him feel twice that.

He'd stayed in the city, working in the little hole he and his twin brother called an office until past midnight, trying desperately to figure out how their struggling rodeo stock company could actually make enough to keep them in the black. It wasn't an easy task by any stretch of the imagination.

He didn't want to admit that he'd also planned his arrival at the ranch long after everyone had gone to bed so he wouldn't need to spend the evening awkwardly avoiding any situation where he might find himself forced to make small talk with someone.

There was one particular someone he'd managed to mostly steer clear of for months. He wasn't sure this time he would be so lucky.

Diego tried to push thoughts of Kate out of his head. He was home for the Fourth of July because Ma and Pop wanted all their children together, and he had to admit he'd been absent enough over the past six months to feel guilty about it. A few hours here and there, but that was it; now he was going to be there for *days*. His parents were ecstatic. They couldn't understand why keeping a business afloat meant that he needed to disappear from their lives.

He'd never mentioned to them that he was completely infatuated with Kate Andrews, the beautiful, intelligent, fiery woman they'd hired to run the ranch's riding school. The woman he had immediately been drawn to the first time he'd seen her, and hadn't been able to get out of his mind since.

The woman who also happened to be dating Jose, his twin brother.

Diego took a deep breath. He'd just avoid her as much as possible, pretend like he didn't worship the ground she walked on, spend some time with his family, and then get back to his office, where a desk full of paper-work waited for him. He could do that, right?

He would simply have to. There was no other solu-tion.

He stepped out of his truck and breathed in the dusty heat of a Texas summer. Even this late at night, the warmth wafted from the ground that had baked all day in the July sun.

It was long past time to go to bed, and Diego looked forward to sleeping in late the next morning, staying out of Kate and Jose's way, and eating too much bar-becue with his friends and family. If he played things right, he wouldn't even need to talk to her, which was best for everyone, really.

Diego crept into the house, trying to be as quiet as possible. The moment he stepped inside, though, it was apparent he wasn't the only one up at this late hour: the doorway to the kitchen glowed a warm yellow, and he could hear the quiet scrape of a ceramic dish on wood. Diego smiled to himself. There was no question in his mind whom he would find when he walked into the cozy light, and it was someone he very much wanted to see.

"Hi, Ma," he said to the gray-haired woman standing beside the kitchen table as he stepped into the bright kitchen. She had evidently just finished setting a steam-ing plate of chicken and mashed potatoes at his usual seat, and she straightened up with a grin.

"There you are, dear!" she said in a hushed tone as she hurried over to hug her son.

Diego embraced her, feeling some of his weariness fall away. Even though he and Jose were adopted, Ma had always been the most devoted and doting of mothers one could ever hope for—far better than their biological mother, a lesson they'd learned the hard way years before. Ever since that disappointing reunion, Diego made sure Ma knew just how wonderful he thought she was.

She squeezed him tight before ushering him toward the meal. "You must be hungry. And exhausted. You've been working yourself too hard, Diego. I expected you hours ago," she told him.

"You didn't need to wait up for me," he insisted, but she dismissed his words with a wave of her hand.

"I've had plenty to do preparing for tomorrow. I've never had so many people over for a holiday before, and if I didn't do some of the work now, I'd be running around like a chicken with its head cut off all day tomorrow."

The wrinkles around her eyes creased as she smiled at the prospect. With her two older children settled down so recently, and both of them living back in Spring Valley to boot, Ma was just about over-the-moon with happiness. She'd invited half the town over for the holiday festivities, and he'd bet that was just so she could show off her abundance of family.

Diego thought about his brother Brock, married, living next door, and now the father of young twin boys; and his sister, Amy, so pregnant she was about to burst and living just a few miles away with her new husband. And, of course, Jose was with Kate, a woman his parents absolutely adored.

How Ma managed to keep from floating right off the ground was anybody's guess.

Diego felt a twinge of jealousy, but he tried to stifle it. He was happy for his siblings, there was no doubt about that. He just wished—

"Eat up and then get to bed, dear. Brock said they'd all be here bright and early for breakfast," Ma said as she placed a hand on his shoulder, breaking him out of his thoughts. "Oh, and you should sleep in Amy's old room tonight and let Jose alone. You know how he hates getting woken up."

Diego wondered if Ma was purposely naive in assuming Jose hadn't snuck into Brock's old room, where Kate slept, but he said nothing. He just picked up his fork dutifully and started to eat. The food was rich and delicious, as anything with that much fat and butter had to be, but it was still hard to swallow with that thought in his mind. While he worked his way through the mound of calories, Ma sat down across from him. "Speaking of Jose, you haven't talked to him about leaving the business yet," she said.

It wasn't a question, more of a prompt. Diego swallowed his mouthful. "I can't ditch him," he told her, keeping his eyes on his plate. Ma just raised an eyebrow at him. "We'd be flat broke if I left now. Besides, it's the summer. This is our busiest time. Jose needs me. It's not that bad, really."

He didn't need to hear her thoughts to know she considered everything he said a load of excuses. Maybe she was right, but it didn't change the fact that Diego would stick with the rodeo stock business, arranging deals between ranchers and rodeo organizers from behind a desk in a tiny office that made him feel claustrophobic, until Jose got bored of it. Just like Diego did with each one of Jose's ventures. Ma shook her head a little. "I love you and Jose both dearly, Diego, but you can't always protect your brother. I know you wouldn't be broke in the first place if he hadn't sunk so much money into that fool plot he thought was a 'sure thing.' And I know you're working yourself to the bone on a business you don't enjoy. It ain't right, son."

Diego shrugged. He knew all this. "But it's Jose," he said, so much meaning in those few words.

Ma nodded as if this made sense to her, though Diego knew she didn't really know the half of it. Jose and Diego were identical twins, brothers and friends from birth. Diego knew that Ma didn't understand his stubborn faithfulness to Jose and his many schemes. She didn't know about the search for their real parents or the promise Diego made the day they'd met them all those years ago. She didn't know about the times Jose had saved his life. He owed his brother so much.

Diego would do anything for his brother and would never hurt him if he could help it. They were a team for life.

As difficult as it was to constantly pick up the pieces while Jose bounded through life in his carefree way, Diego couldn't imagine leaving his brother to fend for himself. Diego had always been the responsible one, and Jose needed him.

Ma said nothing more on the subject. She just stood

and gave Diego a kiss on his cheek as she picked up his plate. "You get to bed now," she said.

Diego stood up with a weary groan and left the bright kitchen. His eyes slowly adjusted to the shadowy darkness as he pulled himself up the stairs, feeling like every bit of energy had been drained from him. He'd been on edge for so long, and now that he knew he wouldn't be seeing Kate until the next morning, he was left feeling exhausted and, though he hated to admit it, a little disappointed.

He put his hand to the doorknob of the room he'd shared with his twin since infancy, then thought about what Ma had said. She was right, Jose hated getting woken up. And if he *was* in Kate's room, well, Diego didn't want to see the empty bunk and know it for sure.

So Diego walked farther down the hall to Amy's room. Her bed was a little short for Diego's long frame, but it would do. He slipped into the dark space, dropping his clothes in a puddle on the floor. He didn't bother to turn on the light. He was too tired to do more than strip to his boxers and climb into bed, his mind fogging over with drowsiness before his head even hit the pillow.

After a long, deep, dark sleep, Diego found himself experiencing a spectacular dream like none he'd ever had before. In it, he was experiencing a mind-blowing kiss that set everything about him on fire. He could *feel* the soft, supple lips of the woman pressing against his as he moved his hands through her silky hair and down along her neck and shoulders. He hoped it would be a long time before he awoke and she disappeared.

It took him several seconds to realize he was already awake, not in a dream at all, and that the lips and hair were connected to a real, actual person.

He bolted upright and turned on the light, then stared dumbstruck at the woman lying in bed beside him with full, just-been-kissed lips. He knew that deep red hair, those freckles dotting her nose in a way that somehow made her both look feisty and irresistibly sexy.

It was Kate. He had been kissing Kate. His mind couldn't wrap around what had just happened.

She was breathing hard, her face flushed, her lips turned up at the corners into a smile that made it clear she'd enjoyed the kiss as much as he had. Her hazel eyes stared unabashedly up into Diego's brown ones, and he found himself unable to pull his gaze away from hers. Diego's heart hammered away inside his chest.

"Am I asleep?" he asked aloud, trying to come up with any other possible explanation for the situation before him. None of this made any sense.

Her smile widened into a full grin that only made his heart beat harder. "You seem pretty awake to me," she said breathlessly, brushing back her mussed hair. "That was…wow."

Diego felt hope bloom in his chest, despite everything. Did she have feelings for him, too?

Kate sat up and looked toward the door. The bed sheets slipped to her waist, revealing a tight white pajama top that left far too little to the imagination. "You shouldn't be here, Jose," she whispered.

Diego's heart plummeted as he realized her mistake.

Kate shook her head in admonishment. "I gave up my

room so you could stretch out, not so you could sneak in here in the middle of the night. You know how I feel about behaving appropriately in your parents' house."

The reality of the situation wasn't pretty, and it took Diego another few seconds to find his voice. "I'm not Jose," he finally managed to get out.

The smile dropped from Kate's lips and her eyes opened wide. She looked as shocked as he felt. "Diego?" she asked quietly.

Damn. He didn't know what he expected, but her reaction still hit him in the gut.

Diego nodded. Kate, Jose's *girlfriend*, covered her face with her hands. "Oh, my God, you're Diego," she groaned.

Her extreme embarrassment broke Diego out of his frozen state of shock. "I'm so sorry," he blurted out in a rush. "I thought this room was empty and—"

And I never expected to find myself kissing the woman of my dreams, he finished in his thoughts.

Kate shook her head, still not looking at him. "It's not your fault. I just assumed..."

She trailed off, but Kate didn't need to say what she had assumed. Everything seemed very clear to Diego. She assumed her boyfriend had snuck in to spend the night with her. Her boyfriend, who happened to also be Diego's identical twin brother.

"I'm going to go," he mumbled, not sure what else there was to say.

Before she could respond, he grabbed his clothes from the floor and rushed out, not looking at her again. Once he was safely in the hallway, though, Diego stopped and leaned against the closed door, allowing himself a few deep breaths. They did no good. His heart was still pounding like he'd run a marathon instead of dashed out of a tiny bedroom.

His attraction for Kate before was nothing compared to his feelings now that he'd kissed her, held her in his arms, and he let out a deep sigh.

Dammit, Jose, he thought as he walked to his and Jose's apparently empty room. *You have all the luck.*

If he didn't have the deeply instilled belief that Ma would somehow find out if he did, he would have cursed her, too. He was sure it had been an innocent mistake, but her innocent mistake had just stuck him into a whole heap of trouble.

Kate stared at the closed door, fighting the mad urge to rush to it and chase after Diego.

That kiss. She could still feel the pressure on her lips—intense, full of desire, but still somehow tender.

Jose's kisses were always hungry and demanding. Nothing like what she'd just experienced. She should have realized immediately that it was Diego. She'd only met him a few times, had hardly spoken to the man, but it was enough to know that he and his brother were as different as night and day, however much they looked the same.

Kate groaned quietly and dropped her head to her pillow, then turned her face so she could see the bedside table, where a diamond ring sat, its facets glinting at her in the lamplight. This was very, *very* not good.

It was nearly morning, and Kate punched her pillow

a few times and tried to lie down and close her eyes, but there was no way she could get to sleep after what had just happened, even though she had been up much too late—first at the rodeo, then agonizing about that damn ring on the nightstand and what would happen when she gave it back.

She tried to read a bit to get her mind off the whole big mess she found herself in, but after a few minutes she gave up and paced aimlessly around the little room, feeling cooped up, but too nervous to leave the room. What if she met Diego in the hallway? Or Jose? Or, God forbid, both of them?

Nope. Better to wait and make a dash for downstairs once other family members had arrived. She definitely needed a buffer around when she saw either of them. The conversation she needed to have with Jose would have to wait. Once again, she berated herself for not breaking up with Jose when she had the chance. Her efforts to let him down easy had really come back to bite her.

And Diego, well…if all went as she hoped, her next conversation with Diego would be somewhere in the vicinity of never ever. She was far too embarrassed to be around him.

Embarrassed, she repeated to herself. Certainly not attracted, like some parts of her body seemed to believe.

She got dressed slowly, listening for noises below, and wished like hell she'd come up with some other way to spend the Fourth of July. Even a lonely hotel room would be better than this. And then she would've missed the rodeo the night before, too, and this entire debacle could've been avoided. If only, if only.

For the thousandth time in the past two hours, she replayed The Kiss. It had already earned capital-letter status in her mind, the standard by which all other kisses would be compared. A mostly asleep touch of the lips that had quickly deepened into a connection that made her heart stutter.

For a moment, it had given her hope that her problems had been solved. Some of her commitment to breaking up with Jose dissolved in those few seconds—the sweetness behind the kiss made her suddenly sure there was a side to Jose she'd missed, and the relief she'd felt was almost overwhelming. He was more than just a joker, a guy wandering through life without letting it touch him. And she had thought for a tiny happy sliver of time that perhaps they'd be able to make it work after all.

Kate didn't want to admit, even to herself, how thankful she'd been. She loved this job so much, had grown so fond of Ma and Pop, and she knew she might need to leave when she and Jose split up. It had made things that much harder over the past few months as she'd started to realize Jose wasn't the right guy for her.

It had even gotten to the point that she was glad he didn't come to Spring Valley very often because she wanted to put off the inevitable breakup as long as possible. In fact, she'd been convinced, just by his absence, that he felt the same way and didn't know how to break things off, either. So she had finally decided that this was the do-or-die weekend, only to have her moment thrown back at her in the most unexpected way when Jose proposed.

If it had been him who'd kissed her like that, though…

But no, it had to be Diego who made her heart pound right out of her chest. And really, Jose *couldn't* have kissed her like that. She had known the truth for weeks now: she and Jose didn't make sense and never would, and that was why their kisses never set her on fire like that. But Diego was different.

It was incredibly clear to her that the chances of keeping this perfect job working with the McNeals had gone from slim to none in the time it took for her lips and Diego's to touch.

Kate was broken out of her reverie by a knock and shouts from below, followed by the murmur of conversation and the pounding footsteps of young children. Finally, she could escape this room and distract herself from her own thoughts.

After a quick glance through the cracked door to double-check that the hall was empty, she walked quickly to the stairs and made her way toward the living room without a pause.

Whatever had happened a few hours before, she wasn't going to let it ruin the holiday for this sweet family who had welcomed her with open arms. She would just try to avoid being too close to either Jose or Diego. If she could sidestep any awkward situations, things would be just fine.

After one more fortifying breath, Kate walked into the living room. She was about to say, "Happy Fourth of July!" but only managed the "Ha—" when a voice shouted her name so close behind her that she nearly jumped out of her skin, cutting off the rest of her statement.

Before she could recover, she was wrapped up in someone's arms and being lifted off the ground. Kate's jolly greeting ended as little more than a squeak and a gasp for breath.

"Set her down, you idiot," Brock said from his spot on the floor, where he and his young stepsons were building a block tower.

"Excuse me for being *romantic*," Jose shot back as he finally set Kate back on her feet.

Kate rubbed the place on her arm that ached where he'd squeezed her but bit her lip and said nothing. Now was not the time to explain to Jose what the word *romantic* meant. She flushed, feeling embarrassed and annoyed.

"How are you, Kate?" said Cassie, Brock's wife, as Kate sat beside her on the sofa.

Cassie and Kate had become friends almost as soon as Kate moved to town, and she knew that Cassie, the town's doctor, was unusually perceptive. But this wasn't the time to get into her worries or discuss the events of the last twenty-four hours. She mustered everything she had in her to give Cassie a sincere smile. "I'm fine, Cassie. How are you?" she asked, as convincingly as she could.

Cassie's eyes didn't move from Kate's face, and she knew Cassie wasn't totally convinced. Kate shrugged. "There are a lot of changes going on and it's just a bit…overwhelming," she said softly, not wanting Jose to overhear.

Cassie nodded and gave Kate a quick side-hug—she had been at the rodeo the night before and had watched the proposal firsthand—and then focused her attention on the boys playing on the floor. They'd switched from building towers to knocking them down with as much force as possible.

Kate was glad Cassie's eyes were off her, and she took a deep breath. She had a sneaking suspicion Cassie was at least somewhat aware of Kate's tangle of emotions regarding the ring upstairs—the one Kate couldn't force herself to actually wear.

In fact, Cassie had seemed more quietly sympathetic than excited about the whole event the night before, and Kate wondered if it might be best to open up to Cassie and ask for her help. Though how Cassie could help her in this situation wasn't at all clear to Kate; she had no idea. Still, it could be good just to have somebody to talk to about it all.

Her thoughts were cut short by Diego's entrance. Kate tried not to stare at him, but it was hard. How could she have ever mistaken him for Jose? Yes, they were identical twins, both tall with bronze skin, coffee-colored eyes and jet-black hair, but everything else about them was so starkly different: Diego didn't have any of Jose's joking swagger, and his eyes were kind rather than perpetually amused. He didn't have that smirk Kate had come to recognize as Jose's trademark.

The more she noted the differences, the more she'd wished she hadn't gotten involved with Jose in the first place. When she'd moved to town, Kate had been so worn down from her old job and from being alone that he seemed like the perfect antidote. She just needed to have some fun, and the man was definitely fun—and, as a bonus, quite attractive.

She should have realized that in order to be truly happy she needed someone who brought more to the relationship than fun and good looks. Kate just wished she'd figured that out before getting herself into this sticky situation.

And now she'd found the whole package, and he was completely off-limits.

Chapter 2

Kate watched Diego as he entered the room and greeted his family members, each one of them genuinely happy to see him. When he got to her, he gave her a cursory head bob and hardly looked at her. If she didn't see how his ears flushed pink, she might have thought he was angry with her. But that coloring was definitely from embarrassment, not anger. He settled onto the floor next to Brock, folding his long legs in front of him, and immediately began playing with the kids.

Her heart started to melt as she watched the children light up with excitement over their uncle's attention. It took a good deal of effort for her to rein in her wayward emotions.

"Ma said you didn't get in until after two in the

morning," Brock said, shaking his head in protective-older-brother disapproval. "Are you planning to work yourself into an early grave?"

Jose walked over and slapped Brock on the back of the head, grinning widely. "Hey, if he doesn't keep at it, our business won't make it through the first year. We all have to make some sacrifices."

Brock rubbed the back of his head and looked up at Jose. "What sacrifices are you making, exactly?" he asked, his voice dripping with sarcasm.

Kate could feel the tension in the room mount as Diego looked from his twin to Brock. She wondered what Jose could say to that; after all, she'd been with him long enough to see that he wasn't sacrificing much at all to build up his business. Not compared to the effort Diego was putting in, apparently.

Jose smiled, but this time, the smile had a tinge of anger to it, and Kate waited for the sharp words she knew were coming. She'd seen him lash out a few times, like once when a man at a bar had hit on her, and she hadn't forgotten how cruel Jose could be when angry.

Before either man could say another word, Diego placed himself between them. "Cool it, guys," he said, looking from one to another before his eyes settled on his twin. "Jose, let's go see if Ma needs help in the kitchen."

Jose looked for a second like he might stay and argue, but after a moment he nodded and followed Diego out of the room.

As soon as they were gone, Brock looked at his wife, who was shaking her head slightly at him. "I know, I know. I promised not to say anything. I just worry about Diego," Brock told her.

"He's an adult. If he wants to get out of this thing, he'll need to do it himself," Cassie said in a half whisper. It sounded to Kate as if they'd had this conversation more than once before.

"But Jose—" Brock began, only to stop abruptly when Cassie cleared her throat.

Brock glanced at Kate for a second, then looked away. "All I'm saying is that they need to be on the same page," Brock finished.

Kate felt awkward as she realized Brock had been about to say something harsh about Jose, but after Cassie's reminder that Kate was in the room, he had tried to avoid disparaging Jose in front of her. The conversation came to an abrupt end.

Kate considered telling them that she was well-aware of Jose's faults but decided against it. It was a holiday, not a time to sow more discord among a family she cared for deeply.

At that moment Amy and her new husband, Jack, appeared at the door, wide grins on their faces as they surveyed the assembled group. "Looks like we're the last ones here," Amy remarked as she waddled through the door with Jack walking beside her as if he was guiding her over dangerous terrain, until she reached the biggest, squishiest chair in the room. Her belly stuck out in front of her as if she'd stuck a beach ball into her shirt.

Kate couldn't believe how large Amy had gotten. She was a couple of days past her due date, and it seemed impossible the baby was still refusing to join the world.

From the looks of things, that kid was using up every possible inch of space.

Jack gathered a few pillows and arranged them to create a pregnant-lady-nest before helping Amy into the chair. Amy gave him a thousand-watt grin in return. Every time Kate was around those two, she felt an ache in her heart as she saw the love and devotion they heaped upon each other.

Diego would probably treat a woman like that, she thought before managing to clamp down on the thought.

"How's the riding school going, Kate?" Amy asked, turning to her. She and Jack had recently changed their competing riding school into a rodeo ranch, but Amy still had a soft spot for the younger children and liked to keep up on what was happening over at the McNeals'.

Kate was happy to have something else to do besides think. Thinking had suddenly become very dangerous. "Since we got the kids from Jack's school," she said, nodding at Amy's husband, "business has been up. Even more so now that it's summer. I'm sure it's still not as busy as it was in Spring Valley's heyday, but it gives me and Pop more than enough to do between the two of us."

Amy nodded. "That's good to hear. Maybe one day soon Spring Valley will go through a boom and Pop will need to hire even more instructors like you. Though from what he tells me, that would be awfully hard to find. Pop still can't believe his luck that Jose found you."

Kate didn't know what to say to that. The elderly Mr. McNeal had almost immediately made his way into her heart, was the sort of kindly father figure she had wanted in her life for as long as she could remember.

The thought of disappointing him, of leaving this ranch house that had begun to feel like home, hurt more than she wanted to admit. Her time at the ranch seemed like it could be near an end, and that thought created a ball of sadness that lodged in her chest.

And Diego? Well, it was one kiss that caused a silly momentary infatuation. She'd get over it quickly enough once she left, she assured herself. She'd just need to avoid him and do everything she could to find a way to stay employed with the McNeals while breaking things off with Jose without any hard feelings. How hard could that be?

Well, might as well start packing, she thought with a little eye roll.

If there was any possibility she could make all that happen, though, then any ideas about a relationship with Diego had to be ignored, because there were exactly zero ways *that* could work out. Things were difficult enough without throwing that in, too. At least she wouldn't see him all that much as she got over her little crush. He almost never came home for visits lately, a new development that Ma complained about to no end. Apparently, it had started…

Just after she came to work at the ranch, she realized.

As if he'd been avoiding *her*.

The realization hit her like a pile of bricks. Did he have feelings for her even before they'd ended up in the same bed?

No, it couldn't be. She was reading too much into things because of her crush.

Teeny-tiny nothing crush that would go away in a day. Her silly infatuation.

At that moment, Jose and Diego walked back into the room, and Kate felt her breath catch in her throat. Diego glanced at her, and his eyes told a story she didn't want to read.

No, she *had* to be making all this up. Silly infatuation, she reminded herself as she stood and headed out of the room. She needed some fresh air.

"Hey, where're you going?" Jose asked before she could disappear. "Ma doesn't want any help. I already checked."

"Taste-testing isn't exactly helping," Diego said quietly, but Jose ignored him.

"I need to check on the horses," she told Jose, purposely keeping her eyes off Diego. "They haven't been fed or watered yet this morning."

"It'll have to wait until after you eat," Ma said as she appeared beside Kate and put a hand on her shoulder. "Everything's hot, and you need some victuals before you start working up a sweat out there in the heat."

There was nothing for Kate to do but allow Ma to steer her toward the table. The rest of the family followed, and soon they were all crowded around piles of eggs, bacon, hash browns and a giant stack of flapjacks. It looked like enough to feed an army, but Kate guessed the table would be empty soon enough, by the way the McNeal children were piling it onto their plates.

Everyone except Diego. Even Amy was attacking the meal with more gusto than he was, but to be fair, she was so pregnant that her appetite was no surprise.

Diego's lack of a large appetite, though, seemed odd. He was picking at his food in a very uncowboy-like way. Almost as if something was weighing on his mind.

She didn't really want to examine it too much, and silently hoped for a distraction. Like a tornado, or Amy going into labor, or—

"So, how was the rodeo last night?" Ma asked the table of children and spouses. "Josc wouldn't say a thing when he and Kate came home."

Not exactly the distraction Kate had been hoping for. She could feel every muscle in her body tense as she waited for someone to speak. It shouldn't have been surprising, but it hadn't occurred to her that it might come up over breakfast. She should have spent her early morning hours deciding how best to stop this freight train. Too late now.

Brock and Cassie looked at Jose expectantly. They'd been at the rodeo, too. They knew what was coming.

Kate wished she'd thought of what to say and had the guts to say it when the announcer at the rodeo the night before had thundered Jose's proposal across the crowd. But she'd been so stunned and there were so many people looking at her that she'd stayed quiet when Jose slipped the ring on her finger and pulled her into an embrace. It wasn't a *yes*, but that didn't seem to matter.

She would need to get herself out of it, but after what had happened with Diego, the best she could hope for was to do so without hurting too many people. And then she'd find a new job and move on once again.

Kate could feel tears stinging her eyes and kept her gaze on her food. Now was not the time to get upset.

She was an optimist, she reminded herself. She'd get out of this…somehow.

Meanwhile, Ma was looking at everyone with growing suspicion as they all silently stared at Jose, waiting for him to say something. "What has got into y'all?" the older woman asked, her voice stern, demanding a response.

Jose, the only one still eating, glanced around at all the eyes on him. "Oh," he said, shrugging in a way that made it clear he was enjoying all the attention. "It's probably because I got engaged last night."

There was a short pause of silence before Ma and Pop were pulling Kate and Jose into congratulatory hugs. "We are so happy for you both," Ma told them, looking at her son. Ma was so quiet she seemed almost on the verge of tears. Kate was worried the old woman was going to start crying from happiness, and that only made Kate feel worse.

For the first time, Kate really wished Ma wasn't quite so sweet and loving. She wanted to tell them the truth, but couldn't bring herself to do it there, in front of the whole family. As much as she hated herself for it, she stayed silent once again.

"Yep," Jose said, breaking the quiet that had filled the room. "I'm settling down. We'll plan the best shindig any of you have seen. Which means I'm going to need an advance on my paychecks, Diego."

At the sound of Diego's name, Kate flushed and looked at him. His face was as pale as hers was red. He didn't say anything, just coughed and nodded before looking down at his uneaten meal. He picked up his fork but didn't start eating.

Kate suddenly felt very confined in the small room, so she decided to extricate herself from the situation. "I've got to take care of the horses now," she mumbled as she rushed for the door, glad for an excuse to leave.

With that, she ducked out the back door and made her way into the already hot July morning, pulling on her cowboy hat as protection from the harsh sun. Kate took a deep breath and let it out slowly. The wide expanse of land and sky surrounding her always brought a feeling of peace, and she let it soak into her along with the sunshine.

She loved the country. After growing up surrounded by city and clouds and rain, Texas had captured her heart in a way she'd never expected. Kate walked quickly toward the barn, eager to see the horses in her care, more so than normal. She wanted to hide from the family and work herself to the bone to try to rid herself of the guilt she felt at not telling the McNeals the truth.

The barn was dim, but warm from the heat of the morning and the bodies of the animals housed there. Kate grabbed a small handful of oats from a barrel near the door and made her way directly to the fourth stall on the left, the same place she started every morning. "How are you today, Darling?" she asked the chestnut foal who was snuggled up to her mama.

The baby had only been born a few weeks ago, and the sweet little thing was Kate's favorite. Luckily, her mother didn't seem to mind Kate's attentions, so Kate spent time with her every chance she had.

Darling trotted to Kate on her spindly legs and immediately pressed her face into Kate's hand, searching for the treat she knew she'd find there. As the foal gobbled up the oats, Kate stroked her head, admiring how much she'd grown in such a short amount of time.

Once the food was gone, Darling turned back to her mother, who watched patiently. Kate gave her a pat on the nose. "You should be very proud, Lucy," she told the dam.

Lucy shook her mane imperiously, as if to show that she was *obviously* proud of her amazing baby. Kate breathed a sigh of relief and went on to her work, picking up a pitchfork and moving toward the hay bales.

She would muck out the stalls later; for now, just a quick meal and brushing for her charges, then a bit of freedom out in the pasture would be enough to keep them happy.

After just a minute, however, she was distracted from her task by loud talking outside the barn and stopped what she was doing. She turned just in time to see the barn door open and Jose and Diego walk in. Jose was talking, and she caught the end of what he was saying.

"...can't expect me to help if you won't," he said to his brother.

Diego looked annoyed and embarrassed, and Kate immediately put the pieces together. Diego had told Jose that he needed to come help her with the horses. Jose, being Jose, refused to go to work while his twin brother relaxed inside.

"I don't know why you'd want to stay in the house,

anyway," Jose continued. "You always jump at the chance to work with the horses."

Kate had a pretty good idea why Diego would have preferred to stay in the house, if the flush across his neck was any indication. Kate's heart jumped at the memory of the kiss before she squashed it down.

She had work to do, and that kiss meant nothing but trouble for her. So she needed to straighten up and do what needed to get done.

"If you two are here to help, the horses need water and a good brush-down," she called over her shoulder, not looking at either twin.

In moments, Diego had attached a hose to a spigot and was walking down the right side of the barn, topping off the horses' water. Kate kept her eyes on the hay, but she could feel Diego's presence as he moved along the length of the barn, even though they were working on separate sides. Jose, however, was off somewhere in the distance, doing only God knew what as noisily as possible.

Soon, Diego was making his way up her aisle, and she could actually feel him getting closer. Kate shook her head slightly and forced her attention back on the task at hand.

"Where are the damn brushes?" Jose called out after a couple of minutes.

"The shelf on the right," Kate and Diego shouted back simultaneously.

Kate, startled, looked over at Diego, who was looking at her in surprise, too. After a second they both smiled. "You spend a fair amount of time out here when you're home, huh?" she asked him.

There was no harm in being friendly, was there? She still hoped to be on good terms with everyone in the family, and that included Diego, didn't it?

A small part of her brain insisted that she was being a fool and only getting herself in deeper, but she ignored it.

Diego shrugged. "I like helping with the animals," he said, not looking at her. He cleared his throat, as if hoping it would clear the awkwardness between them. "It looks like you spend a lot of time out here, too. I haven't seen the stalls so clean in years."

Kate felt a rush of pride. She had put countless hours into the care of these horses, and she knew she'd done a good job of it. "Thanks," she said, trying to keep her gaze focused on the hay in front of her instead of his deep mocha eyes. "Your pop works harder than he should. I don't know how he managed out here without full-time help before I got here. There's always more to be done. In fact, don't refill the buckets in the last three stalls on this side," she told him, gesturing down the line of stalls. "They're due for a cleaning today."

"On the Fourth of July?" he asked, raising one eyebrow.

Kate shrugged. "Horses don't understand holidays."

Diego tried to keep his eyes off Kate, but he couldn't help but glance at her every few seconds. She wasn't just beautiful, she was genuinely great at her job. A quick glance around the barn was enough to make him sure of that. And the way she carried herself, with confidence in her abilities, and the sparkle of love in her eyes as she looked at the animals—it was enough to knock out any cowboy.

Diego glanced back at Jose, who was halfheartedly brushing a black gelding a few stalls away. He hoped Jose had enough sense to see what a catch she was, but he knew his brother well enough to suspect otherwise.

As if to confirm his thoughts, Jose stopped what he was doing and set down the brush he had so recently picked up. "I'm going to see what snacks Ma has. You two coming in?"

Kate shook her head and Jose shrugged and walked off. Diego knew he should follow his brother.

"You can go with Jose," Kate told him. "I can finish this up."

Of course she could. It was her job, after all. And Diego knew that spending time alone with Kate wasn't exactly a smart idea. He should go inside.

Diego picked up the brush Jose had abandoned. "I'll do this row if you do the other side," he said, starting up where his brother had left off.

"You really don't have to," she said.

He completely agreed. "It's a holiday. You deserve a little break as much as anyone" was what he said out loud. "Unless you'd prefer it if I left," he added.

Maybe she would say yes, she would rather do it alone, and then he could run off and hide without any feelings of guilt.

He waited for her answer, which seemed a long time coming. "Thank you for the help," she said at last. "I appreciate it."

He nodded and turned back to the horse next to him, brush in hand.

The two of them worked quickly, and soon they were walking pairs of horses out to graze in the largest paddock. The silence stretched between them, but Diego wasn't sure what to say. Now that they were alone, without a twin brother in sight and nothing to do but walk together, Diego had no idea what to say or do, so he just walked on and wished the paddock was closer to the barn.

"Thanks for your help," Kate said, her voice soft and kind.

Diego nodded but didn't take his eyes from the land stretching in front of him. "Like you said, horses don't understand holidays."

She chuckled and nodded in agreement as they sent the animals through the gate and out to roam. They headed back to the barn in silence.

She was *engaged*. To his *brother*. Diego didn't know how many times he would need to tell himself that before it stuck and squashed the feelings rising in him. Part of him wanted to jump onto the nearest horse and ride somewhere far, far away. Perhaps California would be far enough away to get his mind off Kate, but he doubted it. He might need to take a page out of Amy's book and fly to Thailand.

He heard the back door of the house slam shut and looked up to find his pregnant sister walking toward them. *Speaking of Amy...* She had a large drink in each hand, and he veered away from the barn to meet her. He could see Kate doing the same out of the corner of his eye.

When they reached her, Amy handed each of them a lemonade. "Ma sent me out with these. She said, quote, 'Make sure those two aren't getting so overheated that they keel over from heatstroke and ruin my party,' end quote. Also, she wants you to come inside to hear your jobs for the day."

Diego wiped beads of perspiration from his face and drank gratefully. The heat was intense out in the sun. He looked at his sister, who was resting her hands on her bulging stomach. "If she's so intent on today being perfect, why is she giving *you* chores? I would imagine you going into labor would probably put a damper on things."

Amy shrugged. "Actually, I think she's so anxious to meet the granddaughter that she'd happily send me off to have a baby while she celebrated here with the rest of the town. She might even be willing to miss fireworks if this baby finally makes her debut."

Kate laughed and started chatting with Amy like they were old friends as they all walked toward the house. Diego watched the women, amazed at how close they seemed. Perhaps it was because he hadn't been home much that he hadn't watched this relationship develop. Or maybe Kate just fit in with everyone as easily as Jose did. Diego had never been one to fit in right away, and he'd always admired the trait in his brother.

In fact, it was probably one of the things that had brought Jose and Kate together. An evening at a bar, laughing, feeling completely at ease—of course they'd found each other. Meanwhile he'd be the guy alone near the end of the bar drinking a beer while working on paperwork for their damn business.

Diego was glad he hadn't eaten much at breakfast, because his stomach had started turning over at the image.

They entered the living room, where almost everyone was gathered, waiting for Ma to arrive and give them each tasks for the day. Jose sauntered over to them.

"Are you both staying for the whole long weekend, Jose-n-Diego?" Amy asked, running their names into a single word, like she had always done as a child.

Jose nodded. What had seemed like a much-needed break now sounded completely exhausting to Diego. Three full days watching Jose and Kate being all engaged to each other wasn't exactly appealing.

He made a snap decision. "Actually, I'm only staying today. I've got a ton of work to do back at the office," he said, feeling both relieved and pained as he said it.

It wasn't a lie. Sure, it *could* wait, but he did have piles of paperwork sitting there waiting for him, and the sooner he got to it, the better for the business. He ignored the fact that he would actually love to break up said business and cut their losses as soon as possible, not put *more* time and effort into it.

"What's that you said?" Ma asked sharply from the doorway, making it clear she'd heard well and good what Diego had said and that she didn't like it one bit.

He looked at her apologetically. "I'll try to come back for a few days in a couple weeks, once things settle down a bit," he said.

Maybe by then he would be able to accept that Kate

was going to marry Jose and they would get to live his happily-ever-after. But he doubted it.

Ma didn't say anything, but Diego could tell by her expression that she wasn't pleased. He was sure that if she could have her way, all of her children would move back home, spouses and children and all.

"Nearly the entire town will be coming out to celebrate the Fourth with us. Y'all got a couple hours to do whatever else you like, but by noon I expect tables and chairs to be ready," Ma said, pointing to her children. "I'll set out an early lunch around ten, so you can snack on a little something before you get to work."

Jose stood straight and saluted. "Sir, yes, sir!" he shouted.

Ma nodded at him before starting to give out jobs.

"Pop, you'll set up the barbecue, won't you?" she said, though it was clear she wasn't actually asking, and she didn't wait for any response. "Kate, I want you to get any work you need to do finished up this morning so you can have a good time this afternoon. If I had my way, you'd take the entire day off, but—"

"Horses don't understand holidays," Kate and Diego said at the same time.

Ma nodded, everyone else chuckled and Kate and Diego smiled at one another. Diego felt his heart flip. He didn't know if he wanted to run away from her or pull her into a kiss. Or, more accurately, he absolutely wanted to pull her into a kiss, and that fact made running away oh, so appealing.

Chapter 3

After Ma gave a small speech about the importance of everyone pulling their weight—except for Amy, who was told to not pull any weight under any circumstances—Kate headed toward the door, ready to get back to the peace and quiet of the barn and her tasks.

"What needs to be done, Kate?" Pop asked, grabbing his battered cowboy hat off the peg and settling it on his head.

Kate shook her head. "With all the help I've gotten today, there's nothing much for you to do."

He tilted his head. "Are you sure?"

"Absolutely sure. You need to take the day off and enjoy being with your family, Pop," Kate told him.

"It's your family now, too," he replied, giving her shoulder a squeeze. "With or without a ring."

Don't I wish, she thought, but only said, "Play with the boys, relax, have a fun time."

He tipped his hat at her in acquiescence and she strode out the door before he could come up with some reason to work more than he should, just as he did most days.

Pop was a wonderful man, but he had a tendency to overwork himself. She felt like she was constantly forcing him to take breaks for his own good. It hurt her heart to think how much he must have been pushing himself before she got there. He still insisted on completing all the paperwork and accounting himself and attending every single class at the school, but at least he'd passed off most of the heavy barn work to her.

Which she didn't mind in the least, she thought as she looked around the large, quiet barn. Kate started to list her tasks in her mind. First she'd clean the water barrels, then muck stalls and tidy things up. Oh, and she would put the rest of the horses out to pasture for the day. That task was interrupted when Amy had brought them drinks earlier. The water barrels were really a two-person job and would take much longer than usual if she did them alone, she noted. All that and a good long shower should take her right up to when the guests arrived, which suited her perfectly.

It would certainly be best for everyone involved if she and Diego didn't have any more chances to have cute moments together like they'd had in the living room a few minutes before. The part of her that wanted more of those made it very clear to the rest that it was something to be avoided.

Kate walked over to the first of the water tubs and examined it, trying to decide the best way to complete this chore on her own. Before she could begin, however, she heard a bunch of talking and looked over toward the open barn door to see a large contingent of McNeals headed straight toward her.

Brock and Cassie, Amy and Jack, and Diego all trooped into the barn. Kate had a sinking feeling she knew what was about to happen, and she was just surprised she hadn't seen this coming.

"What needs to be done?" Cassie asked her. The group waited for orders.

Kate sighed. The work she'd expected would take hours was bound to be finished in a fraction of the time with all this help, and Kate wasn't sure if she was pleased or not. It was certainly nice of everyone to pitch in, but it left her in a bit of a conundrum. She'd planned to spend a large chunk of her morning in the barn, not hiding exactly, but, well…

Yeah, hiding. Originally she'd actually been looking forward to a reason to hide from the entire McNeal clan. Especially Jose and Diego. Now what would she do with her day?

Oh, well. She wasn't going to turn down McNeal kindness, that much was certain. "We need to haul out and clean these water barrels," she said, gesturing to the three in question. "Horses can be taken out. Stalls can be mucked." Kate shrugged. "I think that's about it."

Immediately the group began to split. "I'll take out the horses," Jack said, making for the wall that held the leads.

"Brock and I will take care of one of the water buckets," Cassie added.

"Where's Jose?" Amy asked, crossing her arms in front of her chest.

Kate looked around and noticed for the first time that he wasn't there. Her attention had been…elsewhere.

"He's trying again to see if Ma will let him be the official taster," Diego said.

Amy rolled her eyes. "It's a wonder that boy doesn't weigh three hundred pounds with all he eats. He should be out here helping, you know."

Diego just shrugged and walked over to another of the water barrels.

Kate looked and realized that she had somehow wound up working with him again and wanted to slap her forehead. How did she keep managing to find herself in such close proximity to this man?

Footsteps told her someone new was entering the barn, and for the first time in a long while she hoped to see Jose. But when she looked up, it was Pop who had walked in. This was just too much. "No, Pop. Didn't you hear what I said earlier? You are taking the day off."

She was ready to continue scolding until he promised to relax, but he put his hands up in a gesture of innocence. "I'm not here to work, Kate, don't you worry. Zach and Carter wanted to go for a ride, and since y'all are busy putting me out of a job, I thought I could take them for a quick trip around the place."

Kate smiled with relief. "That sounds like a great idea," she told him.

Cassie's young twins were two of the riding school's

best students, and a horse ride would be a great way for Pop to feel like he was contributing while he still managed to relax a bit and have some time with his grandsons.

"I'll help you saddle up a couple horses," Amy volunteered, but she was quickly shouted down by everyone around her.

"Don't you even think about it," Brock said, eyeing her bulging stomach as if he was afraid it might pop at any moment.

Jack put his hand on his wife's arm and gave her a kiss. "I'll take care of it, love," he said. For a moment it looked like Amy might argue, but then she put her hand on top of her stomach and nodded.

Cassie and Brock also jumped up to help, and soon the three of them were cinching belts on Chester, Pop's favorite horse, as well as two of the most docile mares for the children, despite Pop's grumbling that he could handle a little thing like cinching a saddle, thank you very much.

Zach and Carter ran in with excitement shining in their eyes, and soon they were chattering nonstop as they mounted the horses and followed Pop out the door.

Kate watched them go with a smile. The old man doted on the five-year-old twins, and her heart swelled with the love she saw in this family. Even though Pop and the rest of the family had known the young boys only a year, since Cassie moved in next door, it was clear that Mr. and Mrs. McNeal had immediately come to see them as their own grandchildren. It shouldn't be surprising, knowing that all four of their adult children had been adopted, but it still took her breath away to see so much unconditional love.

It wasn't something she'd had much experience with growing up.

Kate shook her head a little to push away the negative thoughts and focused on the task at hand. She and Diego managed to empty and scrub the barrel clean without talking to each other. In fact, they worked so smoothly together and he was so competent that no words were needed, which was in some ways worse than conversation. Soon they were setting the container back into place. Kate stood up and stretched her back as Amy walked over with a hose and began filling it with water.

"Sorry I can't be more help," Amy told her, looking a little annoyed at her inability to do anything else.

Kate shook her head at the apology. The idea that Amy was apologizing for not hauling heavy objects or cleaning smelly buckets seemed hilarious to Kate. "You just work on growing that person," she told Amy. "I've had more help today than I know what to do with."

Kate looked around the barn. Diego had started on mucking the stalls with Jack while Brock and Cassie worked on the last barrel. Kate estimated the entire barn would be spick-and-span in a matter of minutes. Then what?

As if Amy heard Kate's thought, she shrugged as she moved over to fill the next bucket. "If I weren't pregnant, I'd suggest we all go for a ride and catch up to Pop and the kids, but seeing as horses are off-limits, I need to come up with something fetus-friendly."

Kate looked over at the very pregnant lady and

shrugged. "I don't think anybody's going to let you do much more than sit and chat until that girl arrives. Still no contractions?"

Amy shook her head. "A few weeks ago I was nervous about labor. Now I just want it to be over and done with. Ma says it's supposed to be this uncomfortable, so the mom stops worrying about the pain and just wants to have a baby already."

Kate silently questioned where Ma, a woman who had adopted all of her children, had heard that. It was probably something passed down from mother to daughter for generations.

Kate wondered if her own mother had ever anticipated her arrival, even if it was just so she could stop being pregnant. Then she pushed aside that notion. That kind of thinking didn't help anyone.

Instead, Kate looked out the barn door at the wide expanse of the ranch. Her eyes skimmed across the fenced paddocks, the waving, long grass and the copse of trees that hid a small stream and some pleasant riding paths. She imagined Pop and the kids were somewhere in there, enjoying the shade.

"They'll probably be heading back any minute. Those kids love to ride, but I'm sure they'll be ready for a snack and some new adventure soon," Kate said to Amy, mostly just to have something to say.

"Having little ones around really does liven things up," Amy replied, giving Kate a little smile that she'd come to recognize as Amy's "pre-mommy" look. It was very obvious that Amy was looking forward to having her daughter for reasons besides feeling comfortable again.

Kate took one last glance and then turned back toward the barn, intending to grab a shovel and muck some stalls before the rest of the group got to all of them first. Then she turned again, her eyes scanning the trees for what she had seen out of the corner of her eye. She felt a hint of anxiety course through her.

There.

A horse had broken through the tree line and was racing back toward the barn at top speed.

Kate squinted, then felt her heart in her throat as she recognized Chester. But he was riderless.

Where was Pop? And the twins?

Her anxiety shifted into full-on worry as she scanned the trees again for any sign of life, hoping the three of them would appear. She watched carefully even as she walked forward to meet Chester.

"Kate, what—oh!" She heard Amy behind her but didn't respond. Her attention was completely focused on the trees.

Two more horses appeared, these ones not galloping quite so fast. And they had riders.

Kate let out the breath she hadn't realized she'd been holding as she saw Zach and Carter riding toward her. Pop was still missing, but at least the twins were safe. She caught Chester's bridle as he rushed up to her; then she put a hand on his neck, trying to calm the gasping animal.

If only someone was there to calm her.

She felt a hand on her arm and looked up to find

Diego beside her. Everyone had stopped their work and was standing around her, waiting for the boys. "It'll be okay," Diego rumbled to her softly.

She nodded, soaking in his cool demeanor as they waited to discover what had happened to Pop.

After what seemed an eternity, the two children arrived and were quickly grabbed off their horses by Cassie and Brock and pulled into hugs. It only took seconds to get the story.

Pop had been playing around, showing them tricks on his horse. Then something had happened—neither boy was sure what—and Pop was on the ground. He was hurt. There was blood and he was holding his leg. He'd told them to go back and get help.

Cassie ran to the barn for a first-aid kit as Brock asked the boys exactly where Pop was. Diego hopped on Chester while Brock and Cassie mounted the other two horses. In a flash, the three of them were off to find Pop, Cassie muttering something about the femoral artery and loss of blood.

Kate watched them go, so stunned she could hardly stand. She stood rooted to the spot until they were far away. She could hear Amy behind her comforting the twins and trying to get more information from them at the same time.

Kate was glad there were others around who seemed to know what to do, because all she could do was watch and hope everything would turn out all right.

During her career, she had seen some pretty horrific injuries, and she thought of herself as pretty cool under pressure, but this was different. This was Pop.

Once the three horses were far in the distance, Kate turned toward Amy, who had an arm around each of the boys. "Don't you worry," she told them as she squeezed them as close as she could over her bulging belly. "Pop will be fine. He's strong and your mom is the best doctor there is."

Kate tried to calm herself with Amy's words. She was right—Pop had to be okay. The thought of something happening to him made her want to drop to the ground in despair, but she refused to believe he was really truly hurt. He was too important to her. In fact, he was a surrogate father to Kate, more loving and sweet than her real dad, certainly. Even though she'd known him less than a year, he was a fixture in her life, steady and immovable. He and Ma—

Kate turned her eyes toward the house, which looked as calm and welcoming as ever. Ma didn't know anything was wrong. Nobody had thought of her during the chaos of the moment. "I'll go tell Ma," Kate said to Amy, glad to have something helpful to do.

"You sure we shouldn't wait until they come back and we know more? It might be a kindness to keep her from worrying if it's not necessary," Amy's husband said.

Kate was about to argue but paused. Maybe she didn't know Ma as well as she thought. She was a newcomer to the family, after all.

"No, Kate's right. Ma will have all of our hides if we know something like this and don't tell her. She's a strong woman and doesn't like to be left in the dark," Amy said, nodding at Kate.

Kate nodded back and took off running for the house. When she opened the door, she could hear Ma and Jose's voices. His was teasing, hers a cross between stern and amused.

"If you stick a finger into that potato salad, I will personally see to it that—" Ma was saying, but she stopped as soon as she saw Kate's face. "What happened?" she asked, setting down the dish towel she had been wiping her hands on. Then she grabbed at the end of the table, as if she knew she would need support to hear whatever Kate was going to say.

Kate kept her voice steady and calm. "Pop was thrown from his horse. Cassie, Brock and Diego went out to get him and bring him in."

Kate wanted to reassure Ma that her husband was fine, but she couldn't think of anything truthful she could say. Ma didn't give her time for platitudes, anyway. In a flash, the older woman was out the door, moving faster than Kate had ever seen. Jose was right beside her.

Kate turned off the stove burner before she made her way out. A fire wouldn't help make things any better.

By the time Kate was back with the small group waiting outside the barn, Ma had her grandsons in a tight hug while Amy was finishing explaining everything they knew.

One of the twins was crying too hard to speak. The other whimpered, "It's my fault. I was the one who asked Grandpop to take us for a ride and now he's hurt. We didn't stay with him or anything."

Ma turned the boy so she could look into his eyes.

"Listen here, Zach. You did absolutely nothing wrong. Pop loves a ride with you two and would have suggested it if you hadn't. And I'm so proud that you two listened to him and came back here immediately just like he told you to. You went to get help, which was just the right thing to do. Your mama can do more for him than anyone."

In the silence after Ma's words, Kate thought she heard something and checked the woods. Finally, after a minute or two, she saw movement and waited, heart in her throat, to see who it would be and what they might be carrying. It was Diego and Brock, and supported between them was Pop, upright and limping. Cassie and the horses were following close behind the trio. Kate swept her gaze over Pop, feeling relief course through her veins. His leg was wrapped, and it looked as if Cassie had made a splint out of a stick. But he was moving and awake, and by the demeanor of the other three with him, it seemed like he was okay.

Kate heard a whoosh of air behind her; it was clear Amy and Ma felt the same way she did and had both let out their own huge breaths of relief.

He was hurt but okay.

By the time they arrived, Ma was standing with her hands on her hips.

"Howie, what exactly were you thinking? Were you *trying* to get yourself killed?" she asked as she looked over her husband, her voice more concerned than angry.

He chuckled through clenched teeth. "Guess I'm not as young and spry as I thought," Pop answered, still leaning heavily on his sons.

Ma snorted her response.

"Broke his leg," Cassie explained to the assembled group, "and he lost a little bit of blood, but nothing else seems wrong. Luckily the gash didn't open the femoral artery. We still need to get him to the hospital for a real cast and some tests just to be sure he's okay. I'd like to ride with him and watch for any issues. And he needs to keep his leg elevated, so he'll take up the entire backseat."

She looked at Ma, and Ma nodded, understanding that there wouldn't be room for her in the vehicle. Ma gestured to Cassie and Brock, who would take Pop. "You three get going. The rest of us will be there just as soon as we can," Ma said.

In seconds, the rest of the family had organized car pools, with Jack and Amy driving the twins and Diego taking Jose and Ma.

Kate grabbed the reins of the horses from Cassie. "I'll get these three settled and hold down the fort until y'all get back," she told Pop, hoping he understood that she was really telling him how much she cared for him.

He gave her a pained grin. "I'm sure you will. Thank you, Kate. I'll be back in a jiffy."

Love and relief coursed through her. He knew. Ma took Kate's free hand and gripped it tight for a long moment. "I'll try to get ahold of everyone due to come over today, but if anyone comes..."

"I'll let them know what happened," Kate said, finishing for her.

With a smile of thanks and a few directions regarding the potatoes on the stove and the roast in the oven,

Ma turned to catch up with her husband. Brock and Diego helped him into the back of Cassie's SUV. Kate watched them go. "I gotta go do a thing," Jose said to her, gesturing over to the group of people beside the cars. "Save me some potato salad, okay?" And then he was on his way to his family.

Kate shook her head. She knew he cared for her and for his family, but that wasn't the kind of response she wanted right then. She wanted reassurance, not humor.

Before he climbed into his own truck, Diego looked back at her and nodded, letting her know without words that he would do everything in his power to help Pop. The look on his face made that clear. She nodded in return, and then he was gone, too, the truck door closing between them.

Kate stood there, alone except for the horses, and watched the cars drive off. Then she turned toward the barn and clicked her tongue to get the animals walking. Soon they were brushed and happy out in the paddock with the others.

Kate had more work to do in the barn finishing all the tasks that were interrupted by Pop's accident, but she looked toward the ranch house. First she needed to deal with the food as Ma had directed. It was just a shame nobody was going to get the Fourth of July they wanted.

She looked at the house again, and an idea began to formulate in her mind. Perhaps she'd be able to give someone the celebration they wanted after all, she thought.

Kate walked quickly to the house, creating a mental list of everything to be done. Her work for the day wasn't anywhere near over.

Diego had to fight to keep from pressing the gas pedal to the floor. He knew Cassie and Brock would get Pop to the hospital as quickly as they could. The rest of them didn't need to rush.

Still, his speed slowly edged higher and higher until Ma placed a calming hand on his shoulder from where she sat behind him. "He's fine, Diego," she said.

Diego took a deep breath and let his speed drop back to the limit.

"Cassie will take good care of him until we get there," she added, settling into her seat.

"How can you be so calm?" Diego asked her, amazed.

He could see his mom smiling at him in the rear-view mirror. "If you had four children like mine, you'd learn to not worry about bumps, cuts and bruises. Or a broken leg."

Diego smiled back at her. It was true that they'd done the drive to the hospital a fair number of times with Pop in the driver's seat.

"It's a good thing you had a responsible kid like me around to keep your life from getting too crazy, right?" Jose asked from the passenger seat, folding his hands behind his head.

Ma and Diego both snorted, and soon all three of them were laughing. Diego gave his brother a quick shove, then leaned back against his seat and relaxed slightly. Jose could always be counted on to lighten the mood in an emergency.

That didn't mean he wasn't worried, though. Diego knew Jose well enough that he was sure Jose cared as much as anyone.

"Have I told you about the time Brock broke his leg? You must have been too young to remember," Ma began from the backseat.

Diego and Jose glanced at each other. They'd heard it before, but neither one said anything and soon Ma was reciting the anecdote, her voice full of love and good humor. Diego and Jose laughed at all the right spots.

When the story ended, silence descended on the car, but it wasn't a tense silence that made him push his foot down on the pedal. This time it was a silence of camaraderie and shared experience.

It lasted for a good long while, but the tension began to return the closer they got to the hospital, and as they pulled into the parking lot, Diego glanced into the rearview mirror at Ma.

As calm as she had appeared for the entire drive, and as much as she refused to admit it, he knew she really was at least a little worried about her husband. Diego wished he could do something to calm her fears the way she calmed his, but there was nothing for him to do except get her into the building so she could be told that Pop was fine.

He desperately hoped.

Cassie greeted them at the door. "Amy, Jack and the boys should be here any minute. Pop's on the third floor, but only Ma will be able to see him for a while. He's in for X-rays and will need to be fully evaluated before they apply the cast. Ma, they should let you in. See Brock. He's waiting for you on the third floor."

"On the drive, Howie seemed okay, I'm sure?" Ma asked with the smallest hint of a quiver in her voice.

If he hadn't been her son, Diego wouldn't have even caught it. Diego wrapped his arm around her. For the first time, Ma seemed almost frail to him.

Cassie gave the older woman a reassuring nod. "He was totally fine, except for some pain, of course. He even told us a story about the time he drove Brock in for a broken leg when he was young."

Diego smiled to himself. His parents were meant to be together, that was for sure.

"I don't think they'll find any other issues, and even the leg looks to be a simple break, the wound a pretty minor cut from a sharp rock," Cassie continued, putting her arms around Ma for a quick hug. "Now go upstairs. Brock is waiting for you," she added, her voice encouraging as she gestured inside.

Diego used the arm still around Ma's shoulders to steer her toward the elevator, but after a few seconds, she seemed to regain her inner strength and he dropped his arm before she had the chance to slap it away and assure him she was able to walk to the elevator just fine on her own, thank you very much. She was a strong woman, and he knew that any weakness she showed was bound to be temporary.

Still, he was determined to see her upstairs, and apparently so was Jose. By the time they were on the third floor, Ma was very much her own self. When Brock greeted her as they stepped off the elevator, she put her hands on her hips. "Why on earth are you up here while Cassie's minding the door downstairs? She's the doctor. What were you two thinking?"

Brock's eyes widened at the verbal assault, but Diego could only shrug at him. They had all learned that a worried Ma could go from sweet to irritated in an instant. Brock held up his hands as if to prove his innocence. "Cassie thought it would be better if she wasn't breathing down Dr. Tisdale's neck, and Pop insisted that she should go wait for you."

Ma nodded but still seemed suspicious of the arrangement, so Brock continued, "His doctor is Rebecca Tisdale. You remember her, right?"

Ma nodded again, more accepting this time. "I'd heard from her mother that she was a doctor. Good girl. Smart as they come, even if she wasn't the best rider."

Diego couldn't remember any Rebecca Tisdale, but he imagined Ma knew her from the riding school. That was how they knew pretty much everyone who had grown up in Spring Valley.

Brock waited for another moment. Then, once he was sure he wasn't going to be berated anymore, he gestured toward doors that led into the east wing of the building. "How about I take you in to see Pop now?" he asked, using the same level of wariness he'd use on an unbroken bronco.

Ma nodded and strode through the door, as if she was looking for some other reason to scold. Brock raised his eyebrows at his brothers and followed her. "Have fun!" Jose shouted after them.

Chapter 4

Hours later, Diego sat with his siblings in the waiting room, keeping true to the room's name. They all waited—talked, read and watched the boys play with a variety of objects, including a makeshift rubber-glove balloon Brock blew up for them.

Ma had dropped in a couple times to tell them what results the doctor was waiting for, and most recently to say that they were going to apply the cast. It had been a long while since then, and everyone was antsy. Brock and the boys had gone to find food for everyone as a way to kill time, but everyone had eaten, and time was still ticking slowly with no end in sight. Diego wanted to get Ma and Pop and take them home.

Diego's thoughts drifted back to the ranch, and to Kate. Always back to Kate.

"So, Jose," Amy said, her voice breaking into Diego's thoughts. "You're engaged now, huh?"

Diego wasn't sure if he wanted to hear this conversation. Still, he turned his attention to his siblings.

Jose relaxed back in his chair with a wide grin. "Yep. I decided to follow your example, just without the bun in the oven. Didn't want to turn into an old maid."

"And because you love Kate, of course," prompted Amy.

"Yeah, sure. That, too," Jose said.

At the casual tone in Jose's voice, Diego felt anger bubble up as it never had before toward his twin. Everyone got pissed off at Jose at one time or another, except Diego, who always managed to see the good in him.

But the flippant way he talked about loving Kate, like he wasn't the luckiest guy in the world and should be worshipping the ground she walked on, made his fists clench involuntarily.

"Finding your soul mate is a big deal," Amy said, clearly trying to get a better answer from her younger brother.

"Soul mate? I'm just happy I found someone that can stand to be around me. Plus, we're a really attractive couple. The wedding photos will turn out great," Jose said, making a camera with his fingers and smiling at it, as if he was taking a selfie.

Diego stood up. He couldn't listen to any more of this. He didn't know where to go, but anywhere would be better than here.

As he approached the door, however, a tall dark woman in scrubs and a white coat stepped into the waiting room. She looked vaguely familiar. He stopped and tried to figure out where he'd seen her before.

"Becca?" Amy asked, looking closely at the doctor.

The woman nodded with a grin. "I wasn't sure you'd remember me. It's been a long time."

Amy wiggled her very pregnant body out of her chair and gave the doctor a hug. Diego realized this must be Rebecca Tisdale, the one who had been in the riding school. Diego didn't really remember her, but Amy clearly did.

"So you're Pop's doctor," Amy said to her old friend.

Rebecca nodded, pushing her dark curly hair out of her face as she turned to speak to the entire group. "I'm happy to report that he's doing well. The break was clean and the cast will help it heal correctly. His leg will be in a cast for a while, but he's very strong and healthy for his age, and his injuries were relatively minor. I usually have to convince folks of his years to get more exercise, but with him..."

"Relaxing isn't exactly his thing," Amy declared.

"Whereas I can relax all day long and be ready for more," Jose added with a grin as he leaned back languidly in his chair.

Dr. Tisdale gave him a wide smile. "It's good to see you still have your sense of humor, Jose, even after all these years."

"See, I keep telling you guys that I'm a delight," Jose said to his siblings.

There was a collective eye roll before they turned back to the doctor. "Are you going to keep him overnight for observation?" Cassie asked.

"I recommended it, but according to Mr. McNeal, he plans on being in his own bed tonight and his son married a wonderful doctor, who he trusts will keep him alive for a long time yet, God willing. So he'll be ready to go in an hour or two. You can all go in and see him now while we work on his discharge papers, and then you can head home and enjoy the holiday."

Everyone stood, and soon Pop's tiny hospital room was filled with people. Zach and Carter started sniffling again when they saw the big white cast on his leg, but Pop's high spirits and the markers he gave them to "make him a work of art" soon had them smiling again.

After a few minutes of chatter, reassurances that he really was fine and exuberant coloring, Ma looked at her watch. "You kids should get back to the house now. I've already let everyone know that our shindig is back on for just a couple hours from now."

Diego opened his mouth to argue that Pop should have a quiet evening at home, and by the looks on his siblings' faces, he wasn't the only one thinking that. But Ma held up a hand to stop him. "Howie insisted. Besides, we invited Dr. Tisdale to join us, so he'll be just fine."

Diego closed his mouth. Apparently there was no use arguing.

"Okay, Ma, thanks for letting me know. Yes, I'll get the pies in the oven. Tell Pop—" Kate broke off, not sure what to say. It seemed odd to say that she loved him, but she did. "Tell Pop I'm glad he's all right and I'll see him in a couple hours."

Kate hung up her phone and looked at the pile of now unnecessary items she had prepared to bring to the hospital that filled the cab of her truck. It included the roast and everything for a large family dinner in the hospital, as well as some big surprises that would cheer up Pop, she was sure.

After finishing all her tasks with the horses, she'd gathered everything, then piled it into the truck. She had just been waiting for Ma to call and tell her they would be there overnight and that she could come visit. Now all her efforts were a waste, and Pop would never see everything she had planned for him.

Or would he? Kate looked into her truck and then back at the house, then checked the time. If she hurried, she could get the pies in and have everything done before anyone arrived. But she'd need to move quickly.

Kate wished for some help, and, of course, the one person she knew would actually be a help was the one person she shouldn't be working with. Yes, Diego would be ready to throw himself into the job and they would get it done in no time.

She could just picture him, those dark brown eyes smiling as he heard what she had in mind...

Stop that, she scolded herself. Kate shook her head to get rid of those thoughts and opened the door of her truck. She couldn't sit here and daydream when there was so much to do.

Jose and Diego drove most of the way without talking to each other. Well, Diego didn't talk, and Jose wasn't so much talking to Diego as filling the silence.

He never could be quiet for long, and soon he was chattering about who knew what. Diego was too lost in his own thoughts to pay much attention, and he was used to Jose's noise. And since Jose was used to Diego's silence, the situation fit both just fine. Neither minded.

Diego would never admit to his brother that this time he was quiet because he couldn't stop thinking about Kate. His attraction to her was unlike anything he'd experienced before, and it was driving him crazy. When he wasn't thinking about Kate, he was thinking about how bad it was that he was constantly thinking about Kate.

Diego wasn't sure if he was glad that Cassie and the twins had decided to squeeze into Jack and Amy's truck, making it unnecessary for him to try to hold up his side of a conversation, or if her presence might have kept him from his ruminations. With Jose's mindless chatter, it was too easy for him to get lost inside his own head. He'd been doing it his entire life. This was one time where he tried to listen to his twin if only to stop the constant cycle of thoughts, but it didn't work.

As they neared the ranch, Diego made his decision: he would need to stay at least a day to make sure Pop was settled back home and then he'd be on his way out of town, as far from Kate as he could get.

Speaking of Kate, he thought as he turned in to the drive and got his first glimpse of the sprawling ranch house, *what has that woman been up to?*

Red, white and blue bunting festooned the house while a ribbon of cheap plastic American flags hung from the roof. Crepe paper encircled every available post and patriotic pinwheels lined the walkway, spinning slowly in the breeze.

"Excellent," Jose laughed. "It looks like the Fourth of July threw up on this place."

Diego parked, and he and Jose walked up the porch steps. Diego silently noted the basket full of silly glasses, flag earrings and beaded necklaces sitting beside the door. But that wasn't all: as they entered the house, Jose and Diego were bombarded with balloons and more crepe-paper decorations. The entire house smelled like baked apples and looked like an America-themed birthday party.

Kate burst into the living room, full of excitement, then stopped in surprise at the two men staring at her. It was clear they hadn't been the people she'd expected to see. Diego watched as Jose ran up to her and wrapped his arms around her in a bear hug. "You pranked Ma while she was at the hospital?! That's my kind of girl. She's really going to be annoyed," he said with glee.

"No, it's not like that," Kate protested.

Diego looked around, and suddenly the truth dawned on him. He smiled as he realized what she'd done. "It's all for Pop, isn't it?" he asked.

She nodded. "Ma said he'd wasted good money on nonsense and the Fourth of July shouldn't look like a toddler's party. He looked so disappointed," she explained.

Diego could almost see what had happened. After all, he'd seen similar acts play out a dozen times in his childhood. Pop had come home from a visit to the local dollar store with bags of whatever caught his eye. It was his worst vice, in Ma's opinion. This must have been one of the times that he'd outdone himself and she had put her foot down about the sheer profusion of cheesy decorations.

"I was going to bring it all to the hospital and throw a miniparty for him there, but then Ma called and said that he was coming home today and the party was still on, so…" Kate said, trailing off as she gestured at the garish decorations.

Diego had to force himself not to kiss Kate. This was exactly the kind of thoughtful, caring thing that set her apart from everyone else. And it was exactly why he should spend as little time around her as possible if he didn't want to get hurt.

He knew it was far too late for that.

"When will they get home?" Kate asked.

Diego had been so absorbed in his thoughts that at first he wasn't sure what she was talking about.

"It could be as much as a couple of hours," Diego told her as soon as he realized whom she meant. "Amy, Jack, Cassie and the twins will be back any minute. Brock's waiting with Ma and Pop and will drive them as soon as everything's done at the hospital." He knew he was rambling but he couldn't seem to stop. "Cassie wants to spend a little time organizing things here to make it easier when Pop arrives."

"Oh," Kate said. Diego nodded, feeling awkward.

Jose rubbed his hands together, wearing his most mischievous grin. "I think I might hide in the bushes so I can see Ma's face as they pull up," he said.

Diego's and Kate's eyes met. Diego hoped Jose would

be disappointed. Either way, he and Kate would both be watching Pop, not Ma.

"In the meantime," Jose said, "I'm going to grab a pair of funky glasses, and then I'd love to know what that delicious smell is, and when I can eat it."

Kate shook her head. "The apple pies are for the party guests. There's a meal on the table if you need something to eat."

Diego turned to Jose, glad to have a reason to get his attention off Kate. "Speaking of the guests, we should work on setting up tables and chairs and the barbecue. People will start arriving soon."

Jose grimaced. "But I need to eat. And we should really take one of the pies. Pie sounds way better than manual labor," he said.

Diego wasn't surprised by his brother's response. He opened his mouth to reply, but Kate got to it before he could. "People who don't pull their weight don't get dessert," she said.

Jose gave an exaggerated sigh. "You sound so much like Ma, it's crazy," he told her. Then he seemed to rethink that. "Or more like Diego, actually. He thinks he's my parent sometimes, I swear."

Diego shoved Jose toward the back door without a word. He didn't mind Jose comparing him to pretty much anybody, but it made his heart ache to be compared to Kate. It was just another reminder of how well they fit together.

Jose didn't seem to notice anything amiss and snagged a mouthful of roast on his way out. They were soon pulling tables and chairs from the storage area of the barn with just his average amount of complaining.

By the time Jose and Diego had pulled two long tables out into the sunshine and arranged them to what Diego hoped was Ma's specifications, Jack and Amy were walking toward them from the house.

Amy gestured toward the house. "Did you see what Kate did?"

Diego said nothing, but Jose shrugged and replied, "Yeah, but she did it for all the wrong reasons."

"Trying to make Pop happy is the wrong reason?" Amy asked, crossing her arms above her bulging belly.

"That's right," Jose said with a disappointed shake of his head. "Her motives were totally pure. She wasn't pranking Ma at all. How unfortunate."

"You should stay out of the heat," Diego told his sister, more as a way to change the conversation than anything else.

Amy turned on him, her arms still crossed. "Don't think you can start telling me what to do just because I look like I'm about to explode, Diego. According to the doctor, I'm not going into labor no matter what I do, so I might as well be out here, unless you have a problem with having a big angry pregnant lady around?"

Diego raised his eyebrows at her minitirade. "I just thought you might be more comfortable inside, but do whatever you like, Ames."

Amy sighed and dropped her arms to her sides. "Sorry, Diego. I'm just getting a little tired of being pregnant. I know you were being nice. I won't be comfortable until this little girl decides to make her big debut, but thanks for trying."

Jack rubbed his wife's back sympathetically and then helped her into a chair he'd grabbed from the barn before joining Jose and Diego. "She's a little touchy right now," Jack said to Diego as they entered the barn and grabbed more chairs. "We saw her doctor at the hospital and did a quick check before leaving. Amy was hoping there would be some sign that she'd be going into labor soon."

"She still looks pretty fat, so I'm guessing it didn't go well," Jose said.

Jack shook his head. "It could easily be another week, and if she doesn't go into labor by then, they'll need to induce her. She's been in a bad mood since we left the hospital."

The three men set down the chairs in a pile near the tables as Amy watched, glowering. Diego hated to see his lively sister so grumpy.

"It must not be easy to carry around another person inside you, but you're doing something pretty amazing, Amy," Diego said.

Amy gave Diego a look that made it very clear it was best not to say anything at all. He got back to work.

The men continued piling up chairs, and soon Cassie, Zach and Carter appeared from the house and began to unfold them and place them near the tables. In no time everything was ready. A large white canopy Ma had bought just for this occasion shaded the tables and chairs, and red tablecloths were held down by plates and Ma-approved decorations.

Amy checked the time. "People should start arriving any minute. Hopefully Ma and Pop won't be too much longer."

"Maybe Ma won't even notice the house if everything out here looks great," Kate said as she set the apple pies onto the tables.

Jack, who was preparing the barbecue in Pop's absence, snorted at that idea. Diego chuckled, but he could see that Kate was starting to get a little worried about Ma's reaction to her decorating efforts.

"It'll be fine, and Pop's going to love it," Diego reassured her.

"I hope she flips out," Jose called from where he sat with his first slice of pie.

"Shut up, Jose," Amy and Diego said in unison.

Cassie's phone dinged in her pocket. After a quick glance, she said, "Well, I hope y'all have finished placing your bets, because Brock texted. They're picking up the cake and will be here in about five minutes."

Diego looked at Kate. She smiled, but it seemed like she was rethinking her decision to go up against Ma in the Great Dollar-Store Showdown.

"Jose, let's get inside and help Kate with whatever food needs to be brought out," he said.

Jose jumped out of his chair as he finished the last bite of his piece of pie. He didn't need to be told twice when it came to food.

"And the barbecue is ready for the burgers and dogs," Jack called after them as they headed for the house.

In the kitchen, Diego watched as Kate pulled bowl after bowl out of the fridge: potato salad, coleslaw, watermelon slices and an assortment of dips, condiments and other miscellaneous items Diego could only guess at.

"Ma really went all-out for this thing," Diego commented as he surveyed the mounds of food that now occupied the table.

Jose laughed, his mouth full of watermelon from the large slice he had snagged. "This is nothing. Wait until you check out the fridge in the basement."

Diego hadn't even known there *was* a fridge in the basement, but he followed Jose and, sure enough, there was a new fridge filled to the brim with drinks, homemade hamburger patties, hot dogs and some towering blue concoction that appeared to be made out of Jell-O.

"Wow" was all Diego could say.

"I know," Jose replied. "Only one Jell-O mold? What was she thinking? Any proper Fourth of July party set in the fifties requires at least two."

"If you make fun of her when she tried so hard for this thing, Jose, you know Brock will absolutely kill you. And I'll help," Diego said.

He wondered if they would ever get too old for insults and threats.

Jose shrugged. "All right, all right, I won't tease Ma if she or Brock can hear me."

Diego accepted that this was about the best he could expect from Jose and started loading his arms full of whatever he could grab, steering clear of the Jell-O.

As the two men exited the basement with arms full of hamburgers, a car door slammed outside. Diego glanced over at Kate, who had stopped in the middle of a last check of the kitchen fridge for any missed items to look in the direction of the door.

All three of them set down their loads and walked toward the front door, Jose grinning, Kate and Diego more nervous.

"Pop'll love it," Diego said softly.

"And Ma will go berserk," Jose added with pure excitement. He was acting like he was about to watch a sporting match of some kind.

Diego would have smacked his brother on the back of the head, but then Brock and Pop walked through the door, Pop's right arm around Brock's shoulder, a crutch under his left. Pop was wearing a silly pair of glasses from the basket, beaded necklaces and a childish grin under his bushy grey mustache. "These are some mighty fine decorations," he said, looking as satisfied as could be.

Ma trailed behind the men, taking in the entire scene in silence. After a moment she said, "Kate, did you do this?"

Kate seemed to get a little smaller, as though she was trying to disappear. "Yes, ma'am."

Diego stood and waited for Ma's reaction like the rest of them, clenching his fists to keep from grabbing Kate's hand and giving it a squeeze. That was probably crossing a line. He mentally willed Jose to hug her or something, but his brother didn't.

Then Ma did it instead. She pulled Kate into a tight embrace. "Ain't you just the sweetest thing? I've been feeling the most awful guilt all day for throwing such a fit over this stuff, and you went and fixed my mistake. Thank you, my dear."

Kate wrapped her arms around Ma and reveled in the hug. She could count on one hand the times she remembered her mother hugging her, and even then it always felt obligatory. This, though…

This was true kindness and caring coming through. Tears welled in Kate's eyes. These people were so good and loving, and moving here felt like moving home.

She hated to think that she might lose it all.

Kate pushed aside that thought. For today, at least, she would just enjoy being with this family and having a job she loved. She would avoid Jose and Diego and pretend that everything was good and life was easy.

How hard could that be?

She didn't have much time to think about how wise this all was, because almost immediately she heard vehicles pulling into the driveway. Ma looked around in a panic. "Brock, you help Pop. You three," she said, whipping around to Kate, Jose and Diego. "Is everything ready for guests?"

They walked into the kitchen together, Kate and Diego telling her what tasks were finished and what still needed to be done, while Jose threw in comments about how disappointed he was in her reaction and lamenting the fact that the pies were already outside and not currently in his reach.

Ma immediately got down to business. "Get some burgers out to Jack and as much of the rest as you can carry, then come back with more help. I'll go greet whoever arrived and ask them to bring an item or two down. I think they'll understand, don't you?"

Kate nodded and did as she was told. Jose and Diego followed suit, and soon Jack was grilling burgers while neighbors and friends made their way toward the canopied area wearing American-themed dollar-store jewelry and carrying an assortment of food.

In no time the tables were groaning under the weight of everything Ma had prepared, and the McNeals were greeting all the arrivals with hugs and exclamations of "It's been so long!" and "How are you, Mrs. So-and-so!"

Kate hung back a little, not sure where she fit into all this. Sure, she'd come to know plenty of the town's residents in the months she had lived there, and the parents of her students were certainly familiar faces, but the McNeals seemed to know each person as if they'd spent their entire lives together—it was a level of intimacy Kate couldn't come close to matching. So after greetings and a hug, she wasn't sure what to do next.

She wished she felt as comfortable, as at-home, somewhere in the world. She'd hoped that maybe it would be here, but a glance at Jose and Diego made that seem nearly impossible.

"It's crazy how practically everyone in town seems to be best friends with each other, isn't it?" Cassie said as she approached Kate.

Kate nodded, unable to think of anything to say.

"When you become part of the family, everyone will treat you just like that, too, trust me," Cassie said with a reassuring pat on the arm before she went off to hug more newcomers.

Hope ballooned in Kate's chest for a split second before she remembered what Cassie was talking about. The moment she recalled the proposal, she felt embarrassment wash through her. Of course, that was what Cassie meant. She had almost managed to forget.

But now that she was thinking of it, she had to wonder if everyone else here was, too. Even if some people hadn't been at the rodeo, this was a small town, and news traveled fast in small towns. She was sure that not a single person would go home unaware of her "engagement."

I never even said yes! she wanted to shout at all of them.

Kate had a strong desire to go hide in the barn for the rest of the day. Or, even better, for the rest of her life.

She went over to where Pop was sitting, his leg propped up on a chair, the cast gleaming white in the bright sunshine. "Hi, Pop," she said, sitting down with a sigh.

Pop smiled at her. His flag sunglasses looked absolutely ridiculous. "This is a mighty fine day, Kate. Thank you for seeing to it that the whole thing went off without a hitch."

Kate nodded. "I should probably go out and check on the water and hay in the paddocks. Things were so crazy today that I didn't do a very thorough job out there," she said, hoping he would accept her reason to duck away from the party.

Pop shook his head. "You always tell me I work too much, and here you are thinking about hay during the party. I'm sure the horses are fine. Spend some time with your fiancé and friends."

That was exactly the opposite of what Kate wanted to hear, but she knew Pop was trying to be kind, so there was nothing she could think of to say. She looked around, trying to find somebody to talk to, a place where she could feel comfortable that the engagement wouldn't come up.

Her eyes landed on a group of kids playing a game of tag. Perfect. She knew most of them from riding lessons, and leaving the crowd to keep an eye on them wasn't antisocial; it was responsible and necessary. What if someone got hurt and no adults were paying attention?

Kate knew she was just making excuses, but she grabbed at the opportunity, anyway. After taking a burger and a soda, Kate walked over to watch the game. With the rest of the party to her back, she finally felt at ease. She was good at being friendly when she needed to be, but even at the best of times she was a bit of an introvert. Now, with all the extra complications tossed in, the less time she spent with adults, the better.

For several minutes, she stood alone, enjoying her self-created job. Then she heard the crunch of footsteps and turned to see Amy coming up beside her. "Who's winning?" she said, studying the kids' game.

Kate shrugged. "Hard to say. Probably Kenny, but only because he keeps throwing other kids in the way of whoever's 'it'."

Amy laughed. "I would get so frustrated when the other kids did something like that. I always felt very strongly that there was a right way to play games, and anything else is cheating."

Kate laughed. She could picture young Amy stomping her feet that everyone was playing wrong.

Amy smiled and shook her head. "I tell you, I almost killed Jose more than a few times because of that when we were kids. He drove me so crazy."

Kate's cheery mood dissipated a little. She wished they wouldn't talk about Jose. He wasn't the one she wanted to discuss. She almost asked if Diego had ever caused such trouble, knowing perfectly well he hadn't but hoping to hear a story or two about him as a child. However, before she could open her mouth, she felt something touch her leg.

"You're it!" Zach shouted before he ran back into the crowd of kids. They all stood and watched her, waiting to see what the grown-up "it" would do.

Kate looked at Amy, who laughed again and shrugged her shoulders. "You better go tag somebody. I'm out of the game due to pregnancy or I'd be running away from you, too."

Kate set her plate and cup down on the ground and wiped her hands on her jeans. "Let's do this," she said to the children, who squealed in delight as the adult ran into their midst, attempting to tag the boys and girls, all of whom managed to run just out of reach in the nick of time.

Chapter 5

Diego sat a little apart from everyone, his eyes fixed on the children and their game. Well, it wasn't exactly the children or the game that had caught his attention. He watched as Kate gave chase, her hair streaming behind her as the hat fell off her head and onto the dusty ground, only to be picked up by one of the girls and placed on her own head. The girl taunted Kate before she ran in the opposite direction at full speed.

Kate raced behind her, laughing so hard that it was surprising she could still manage to stay on her feet and play. Diego found it very suspicious and endearing that she nearly caught several different kids, only to have them move out of her grasp at the very last moment. Almost as if she was *letting* them get away.

"What are you smiling about?" Jose asked, sitting

down beside his twin with a burger in one hand and a hot dog in the other.

Diego felt as if he'd been caught doing something wrong, even though he told himself that there was nothing bad about watching a game of tag. "Do you ever stop eating?" he asked Jose, a little irritated, though he wasn't exactly sure why.

Jose thought for a second. "I don't eat while showering, usually," he said. "And I don't eat in bed, unless it's strawberries and chocolate sauce, and then it has to be—"

"Okay, okay," Diego interrupted, not liking where Jose was headed. He looked at the groups of adults near them. "Where's Ma?"

Jose glanced around for a second, then shrugged. "Beats me. I'm going to go get some more pie," he said as he shoved the last of the hot dog into his mouth and stood up.

Diego nodded, but he was hardly listening to his brother. Where *was* Ma? He expected her to be in the center of everything, bragging about her large and growing family, but he couldn't see her anywhere. More importantly, he couldn't hear her. Even with all the conversations happening, Ma's voice would carry, he was sure. She wasn't exactly a quiet woman.

Diego walked back to the house in search of her, but she wasn't in the kitchen or the front room. It was only when he opened the door to the basement that he heard her.

She was crying.

Diego hurried down the steps. "Ma! Are you okay?

What happened?" he said, rushing to where she stood in front of the fridge and checking her for injuries.

She waved him away, sniffling, and let out a little laugh. "Oh, I'm perfectly fine, dear. I was just coming down to get my Jell-O mold and all the worry from this morning… Well, I simply needed a good cry is all."

Diego's heart ached for her. The fear of losing her husband must have been so real for her after hearing he'd had an accident. He put a hand on her shoulder, but she shrugged and smiled. "It comes with loving someone as much as I love Howie, dear. I can't help but fret for him sometimes, and today was certainly one of those times. Now, that's enough of that. Get out of my way so I can haul this thing outside without dropping it."

With that, she carefully took the blue tower out of the fridge and began making her way slowly across the basement. "And don't even think about trying to help me," she said over her shoulder, as if she could see that he was about to do just that.

He closed his mouth and watched her silently. Ma and Pop loved each other like crazy—they all knew that. Even with the bickering that came from marriage, they had always been there for each other their entire lives. They were a team. Soul mates.

He wondered if he would ever find that.

He wondered if he had already found it, but with someone he could never be with.

With a sigh, Diego turned toward the fridge and grabbed a beer before heading back up the stairs. He really needed it.

As he entered the kitchen, a group of people came in

through the back door with much grumbling and arguing. Dr. Tisdale, this time in jeans and cowboy boots instead of her hospital garb, was leading Brock and Pop over the threshold and into the house. "I'm doing just fine, Becca," Pop said to the woman.

"Dr. Tisdale," Brock reminded the old man under his breath.

Rebecca Tisdale seemed to ignore both of them. "Which way is your room? I'll make sure you're all settled in so you can spend the rest of the evening relaxing," she said.

"I *was* relaxing. Hadn't gotten out of my chair once," Pop mumbled, sounding more like a surly teenager than a septuagenarian.

"In the heat and the sun with dozens of people around. You need to take a break, let your body heal. It's had a rough day," Dr. Tisdale said, sounding more like a concerned daughter than his doctor.

Pop looked as if he might argue more, but finally he nodded and the group trooped down the hall toward the main bedroom, which Diego was thankful happened to be on the first floor of the house. At least none of them had to worry about Pop breaking his other leg trying to get up and down the stairs on his own.

Diego opened his beer and took a long sip. He didn't feel in much of a party mood, but he knew Ma would notice if he didn't come back. Oh, well, he could suck it up for one evening.

As much as Ma disliked his absence, he was sure she wouldn't be very happy with his continued presence if she had any idea what was going on in his head. He sighed and took one more swig of his drink in preparation.

"Diego?" Dr. Tisdale said from behind him.

Diego turned to see the woman and Brock reentering the kitchen, this time without Pop. "Your father asked for you to go talk to him for a few minutes," she told Diego.

He nodded, glad for a reason to stay away from all the celebrating. Maybe he would keep Pop company for the rest of the evening, so the poor fella wouldn't be all alone—

"But don't let him suck you into staying for more than five minutes," Dr. Tisdale warned. "He needs rest."

So much for that plan, Diego thought as he promised to keep it quick.

Pop's room was dim and cool. The old man was propped comfortably in bed with a glass of water and a book on the nightstand. It seemed Pop was expected to stay in bed for a good long time, despite his obvious opposition to the idea.

"Hey, Pop, how's it going?" Diego asked as he walked up to the bed, where the old man was lying with his arms crossed over his chest.

"I'm stuck in this bed and Becca says I have to wear this fool thing for six weeks," Pop grumbled, gesturing to the cast on his leg. "How do you think it's going?"

Diego had to smile at the grumpy response and patted the old man's shoulder. "Dr. Tisdale knows what she's talking about. And it could be worse, you know. I think you should count yourself lucky."

Pop nodded, but he didn't look happy. Then he turned

to his adopted son with as serious an expression on his face as Diego had ever seen. He didn't seem like a surly teenager anymore, but was like an old man. And that was much more worrisome.

"I need your help, son. The riding school is too busy just now for Kate to do it all on her own, and there's no one else around here I trust to run it. I know you've always loved the school and I'd planned to have you take over eventually, anyway. I'm asking you to do that now. I know it's not the most convenient time..." Pop said, trailing off and looking at his cast.

Diego shook his head, even as he knew he would say yes. Of course, he would stay if he was needed. Still, he looked for some way out. "Is there someone else we could hire? Or how about Jose?"

Pop didn't answer, just kept his steady gaze on Diego.

Finally, Diego nodded. He would do anything for the people who had raised him, even if it meant weeks in the presence of the one person he most wanted to avoid. Diego realized the irony of the situation—he was being given the opportunity he'd always dreamed of at the one time he hated to take it.

As if to emphasize how difficult a task Diego was being given, Kate appeared in the doorway as beautiful as ever. The look of concern she wore for Pop went straight to his heart. She gave Diego the fastest of glimpses before turning her attention completely to the man in the bed.

"Brock said you wanted to see me, Pop. Is something wrong?" she asked, her voice full of love for the old man.

Diego felt his chest tighten as she got closer and he took a step back to allow her to approach Pop without getting too close to him.

"I'll be right as rain in a few weeks," Pop assured her, patting Kate's hand as he did so. "It seems like it's a good time for me to retire, though. I know the riding school will be in good hands, with you and Diego here. He's agreed to stay on and take my place running the business."

Kate whipped her head around toward Diego. The expression on her face made it clear that this wasn't the ideal situation for her, either. Diego wasn't sure if that made him feel better or worse.

"Don't worry, Kate. Diego was born to do this job. Everything will be the same, except instead of an old grump tottering around the barn, it'll be a young grump."

Pop's attempt at humor hardly registered in Diego's brain as he stared at Kate, knowing she was as unhappy about the turn of events as he was. She probably didn't want someone new to come in and screw up her way of doing things or put her job at risk, he thought.

But she didn't know how much he disliked the situation, and he was going to keep it that way. He gave her a smile that he hoped didn't look too forced. "Don't worry, I'll try not to step on your toes. I know you do an amazing job around here."

She nodded but still didn't say anything or look much happier. He grasped for something else to say that might ease her fears. "Even if you didn't, I couldn't really fire my brother's fiancée, could I?" he said, going for humor as well as a stern reminder to himself that she was very, very off-limits.

Kate grimaced, and Diego immediately regretted his joke. “I didn’t mean to insult you or anything,” he said quickly, hoping to fix the mess he had made. “I was just trying to let you know that whether Pop’s in charge or I am or anybody else, you’ve got a spot here.”

He stuck out his hand and hoped he’d done well enough. After a second she shook his hand. “I love my job” was all she said.

Diego nodded. Kate was making it very clear that she planned to stick around, so he would just have to get used to her presence. He would do his best to stay out of her way so she could do her job without some lovesick cowboy ruining it for her, even if she didn’t know about the lovesick part.

No matter what he did to avoid her, though, it was a fact that they were going to be spending a lot of time together from here on out, and that was trouble for him no matter how he looked at it.

The next morning dawned bright and clear, and Kate was up with the early summer sun. If she had to work with Diego, at least she could try to avoid working *with* Diego as much as possible. So she was going to get started early enough that she could be done with most of the work before he even woke up.

She was still reeling from Pop’s decision to hand over the riding school to Diego. She had been sure Diego would leave after a day or two and she could get some breathing room to figure out her feelings and try to find a way to continue her employment with the McNeals after breaking off the engagement. Now, however, she was looking at the weeks ahead and seeing nothing but Diego's presence, and Kate could already tell that avoiding Diego was very much in her best interest.

She needed to leave Spring Valley. The way her heart jumped for joy when she heard she would be working with him made it very clear that staying at that ranch any longer than necessary would be a very bad thing.

She'd stay for at least a couple of weeks, until things settled down at the ranch, and then find herself a new position. In the meantime she would do her job as best she could while also steering clear of Diego most of the time.

Leaving wasn't a happy thought, but at least it was a plan. And avoiding Diego was basically a necessity, which was why she was up so very early, sneaking down the stairs, only slipping into her old cowboy boots when she reached the back door.

It was only when she felt the warm morning breeze on her skin that she breathed easier. Everything would go according to plan. For now she would go get some solace by spending time with Darling, the sweet little colt, and work hard. And she would be just fine.

Her relief was short-lived, though, as she entered the barn to find the lights on. Her eyes immediately fell on Diego's long frame. He was stabbing the pitchfork into the hay, then brushing hay from his gloved hands.

He turned her way and his eyes widened in surprise. "What are you doing here?" he blurted.

Kate couldn't help but feel a little insulted. "I work

here," she responded, snapping a little more than she intended.

"No, I'm sorry, I didn't mean it that way. It's just..." He trailed off.

That was when Kate realized he'd been doing exactly what she had planned to do herself. He came out to work early to avoid her. The irony of the situation made her smile.

Diego seemed relieved to see she wasn't angry at him. "Guess we should get this done, huh?" he asked her.

Kate nodded. "What have you done so far?" she asked as she grabbed a handful of oats and went to Darling's stall.

She was happy to have somewhere to look as Diego described all the work he'd done, because otherwise she wasn't sure if she would be able to focus on his words instead of getting lost in his eyes. As it was, she was quite impressed. It turned out that Diego had been up for a good while longer than her, and he had already finished several big tasks that morning. So much so that Kate wondered if he would even need her at all. Perhaps she was just an extra expense for the family at this point and should disappear as soon as possible.

No, she knew her worth on this ranch. She could never do that to the McNeals. Kate was sure she needed to stay on and help, and it had nothing to do with the way her heart thumped as she listened to Diego's deep rumbling voice. She turned toward him and her eyes immediately slid along his body in spite of herself.

"I was just about to get started on mucking out stalls," he said.

Kate returned to reality with a jolt. If there wasn't work to do, she might have run to her room and curled up with embarrassment at where her mind had just gone. She turned away, hoping he couldn't see the flush on her neck, and reached for one of the shovels. "I'll do the left side," she told him as she moved toward the row of stalls, glad to have her back to him.

She listened for a beat, wondering if he'd argue about her taking half of the most difficult job instead of leaving it for him and just adding the fresh shavings or something, as he did the real manual labor. It happened so often to her that she had come to expect it during her years as a ranch hand and horse-riding instructor.

But he said nothing, just grabbed a shovel and moved toward the stalls along the right side of the barn. She shouldn't have been surprised, really—he'd been raised by Pop, after all, and Pop had always trusted her abilities—but it was a rare man in Texas who wouldn't constantly try to protect her from the hard work that came with her position on the ranch.

But not on the McNeal ranch, it seems, Kate thought to herself as she scraped her shovel along the floor of the barn. Just one more reason she would be sad to leave.

Soon she was moving on to the next stall, and the next, wiping sweat from her face as she lifted her shovel and stepped into the fourth. Though the barn was cooler than out in the sun, it was warm enough to make her feel hot and sticky after so much physical labor.

Kate glanced over to see Diego well underway on his fifth stall, a dark line of sweat already staining the back of his T-shirt.

He'd be cooler if he took his shirt off, said a stray thought she couldn't manage to erase. Maybe she was just attracted to him because he looked like Jose, she tried to tell herself. But it was no use. Diego was Diego, through and through, and he was sexy because of who he was, not who he looked like.

Though tall and slimmer than his overly muscled older brother, Brock, Diego had strong arms that made it clear he'd spent more than his share of hours doing hard physical labor. She was sure his chest would be well-defined, and her fingers ached to touch him and see.

Kate shook her head to rid herself of those kinds of thoughts. She needed to appreciate him as a fellow worker, not a hot cowboy.

He worked silently and efficiently, without a word of complaint. Kate tried to use that information to help her create platonic feelings of friendship toward him, but it was no use. That just made him more attractive.

He fascinated her, and she couldn't help it. Kate was sure Jose would have been grumbling up a storm by this time, if he'd even managed to work so long in the first place. It was so strange how different identical twins could be.

Diego glanced at Kate just as she realized she'd been staring at him and should look away. Their eyes locked, and she felt embarrassed for the second time this morning. He had caught her ogling him.

Kate tried desperately to think of something to say that would cut through the discomfort of the moment. She couldn't just stand there looking into his eyes for an eternity without saying anything.

"How are you and Jose so different?" she asked before she'd even realized what she was going to say.

Well, that wasn't great, but it was too late, and it could have been much worse. She might have asked him how it was possible she found him so much more attractive, or asked why she hadn't met him first. Or she could have blurted out a confession that would leave her with no option but to disappear immediately.

Comparatively speaking, her question was not bad.

Diego gave her a little smile, as if he'd answered similar queries a lot in his life. "You can't have two Joses in one family," he said, his voice laced with humor.

Clearly it was something he said often, but that answer didn't seem as amusing to her as she imagined most people would find it. Was Diego the way he was just because Jose was a carefree joker? Was that how he lived his life, as merely the foil to his brother?

Diego seemed to have some idea of what she was thinking. "I think I'd be this way whether or not Jose was Jose. It's who I am, just like he is who he is. We just..."

He trailed off, as if trying to find the right words to explain.

"Make each other more that way," she finished.

She could see how having an impetuous brother could make you even more quiet and responsible than you were by nature. And vice versa.

Kate turned back to the stall and began working again, wondering what it would be like to have so much of your identity tied to someone else. It must be unlike anything she had ever experienced. They worked in silence for a while, lost in their own thoughts, until Diego spoke up from his stall.

"Do you have any siblings?" he asked, his voice drifting over the sound of the scraping shovels.

Kate shook her head, then realized he couldn't see her. "Not really."

"What does 'not really' mean when it comes to siblings?" he asked.

It was a fair question. Usually people didn't notice or care enough to follow up when she said she didn't really have brothers and sisters. "My parents divorced and remarried, so I have half siblings, but I'm not very close to any of them."

"Oh," Diego said. The sound of his shovel stopped, then after a pause, he resumed working again. "What was that like?"

Kate chuckled. She could imagine not having close siblings being a very strange idea to someone with a twin, and the McNeals seemed like they'd always been a close, loving family. She wasn't sure how to answer his question. Finally, she hit on the one word that rang true. "It was lonely," she confessed.

"You never felt like you were part of the family?"

"It felt like I was a reminder of a past life my parents would prefer to forget," she said.

Kate didn't know why she was telling Diego all this. It wasn't something she usually shared. It was probably because it didn't feel like he was asking to pry, but more to understand. And it was nice to be understood. Maybe it had something to do with the fact that she couldn't see him and he couldn't see her as they scraped away at the stall floors with their shovels.

Or maybe it was because the heat of summer always made her think of shuttling between her parents' houses, not really belonging in either. Her mother had always seemed happy to get rid of her for a couple of months, and her father wasn't exactly thrilled to have her show up on the doorstep. Her childhood memories of summer always involved lonely hours spent wandering the city, trying to find a place to belong.

Diego cut through her reverie. "Do you want to talk about it?" he asked.

"Not really," she answered. There was a brief silence. Then the words started pouring out of her. "They both treated me like they were stuck with me. And I never felt as if I was part of the family. The happiest day of my life was when I turned eighteen and left it all behind. I bought a bus ticket the next day and took off. I won't ever deal with cities, snow or disappointing family again."

Kate took a deep breath and realized she'd gotten so wrapped up in her own words that she'd stopped working, and from the silence, it was clear Diego's shovel had stopped, too. She thought she should feel embarrassed going off like that, but actually she just felt freer, lighter. There were a lot of things she'd held inside for so many years, and now that a few of them were out, some of her anger, her resentment, had dissipated and the knot that had long ago lodged inside her felt a little less tight.

"You don't have to respond to all that. Sorry I dumped it on you," she said, returning to her work.

Now that the rush of feelings was easing up, she was glad they were in separate stalls and she couldn't see his face.

"I'm sorry," Diego said, his voice much clearer and closer than it should have been.

She looked up to find him standing in the open doorway of the stall, looking at her with empathetic eyes.

She looked back down and stabbed the shovel at the ground. "Not your fault," she said with a small sniff as she tried to tamp back down the emotions that were roiling in her.

"Yeah," he said, taking a few more steps into the stall. "I'm still sorry."

Kate wasn't sure exactly how it happened or who moved first. In a blur, she was pressed against his chest, his arms wrapped tight around her, and the tears she'd refused to shed as she got on that bus all those years ago flowed fast and hot.

After a minute of silent crying, Kate pushed herself away. She took a shaky breath and tried to pull herself together. Then she laughed a little as she brushed away the last of the tears. "Sorry about that. It's silly to be upset about something that happened so long ago."

Diego watched her with concern but didn't say anything.

Kate turned away from him. She needed to be farther away from this man, whose arms felt so strong and comforting that all she wanted to do was fall back into them. "I'm okay now," she said, not looking at him.

He seemed to understand her need for distance, and she felt more than heard him return to his own stall. Soon his shovel was right back to work. Her heart strained for him, as if they were magnets trying to snap back together when pulled apart. The feeling was unnerving.

"Thank you for being a good friend," she said, as much for herself as for him.

The sounds in the other stall stopped for a second, as if Diego had frozen at the sound of the word *friend*, then resumed. "You're welcome," he replied, his voice almost emotionless.

The stalls were all clean and the day's water barrels scrubbed and filled before either of them spoke again. "Have you talked to either of your parents since you left?" Diego asked when they sat down for a break.

Kate glanced over at him, but he didn't look at her. She turned her eyes toward the far wall. "Nope, not once. They called a lot at first, but I never answered and eventually they stopped."

She waited to hear what he would say about that. She'd made her peace with not having a family a long time ago, or so she thought. But this whole conversation had made her feel unbalanced, unsure. It was a strange feeling for Kate, a person who took pride in her confidence. Around Diego, though, everything was different. He *saw* her.

"They hurt you really badly," he said. She agreed with a nod. "Maybe you should try to contact them, though," Diego added.

She stared at him and he looked right back at her. She thought he'd understood. If they hurt her so badly, why would she talk to them? Why would he even say that?

He seemed to hear her silent questions. "It might

help you get closure to talk to them, hear their side of it, maybe even get an apology. If it's awful, at least then you know you've done the right thing. You tried and now you can move on."

She was about to say that she already *had* moved on, thank you very much, but then she thought about that tight knot she always carried inside her and wondered if he might be right. But the thought of talking to them again, after all these years...

"You sound like a therapist," she said, hoping a little humor would turn the conversation.

Diego picked up a piece of hay and broke it into little pieces, looking as if he was taking what she said very seriously. "I'm not, trust me. But I've had a similar experience before," he told her.

Kate couldn't believe that one bit. She may not be a part of the family, but it didn't seem possible that Ma and Pop were anything but what they seemed. "The McNeals are the sweetest parents in the world!" she exclaimed, wondering how he could possibly compare his childhood to hers.

"Not the McNeals."

She suddenly realized what he meant. "Oh, your biological parents? You contacted them?" she asked.

Diego nodded. Kate absorbed this information. Meeting the people who gave him up for adoption didn't seem to be a happy memory for him. She had so many questions.

"Does Jose know about it?" she asked.

"Yeah, we met them together, just after we turned eighteen," he answered. "He never said anything?"

Kate shook her head. She didn't know why she was surprised, though. Jose never spoke about anything serious. And here was Diego, who hardly knew her, telling her everything with such frank openness.

"It was a difficult experience for him," Diego explained.

Kate wasn't sure that was enough of an excuse, but she didn't say anything about that. She wanted to hear Diego's story. "What happened when you met them?" she asked.

Diego shrugged. "It didn't go well. They seemed kind at first, but then they asked us for money. Jose and I felt betrayed, as if they were getting close to us just for some cash."

"Wow," Kate said. She couldn't think of anything else to say.

"It was hard, and it took me a long time to contact them again. Jose and I had both wondered who our real parents were, constantly thought about if they were going to try to find us, if they'd wanted us, what their story was. After getting crushed like that, I tried to be done, but there was always this feeling of unfinished business," Diego continued.

"So you got back in touch with them, even after what they did?" Kate asked. How could anyone forgive people who would treat their own sons like that?

Diego gave her a little smile. "It took a few years, but I realized how amazing my life is. I've had advantages they could only dream of. Besides, I'm not perfect, either," he said, giving her a significant look that she tried desperately not to read.

"So we worked things out, and I send them a little money here and there," he went on, looking away from her. "The point is, I tried again because I didn't want to spend the rest of my life wondering about the what-ifs. And now I have a better understanding of who I am and where I'm from."

Kate was quiet, soaking in what he'd said. She understood what Diego meant about the what-ifs. She often wondered what her parents were like all these years later, if they would still treat her like an embarrassment instead of a person.

"It seems like you could use a little closure, is all I'm saying," Diego explained before leaning back against the wall, another straw of hay in his hand.

It would hurt to discover that nothing had changed, that she'd been right about them all along, but at least then she could stop wondering.

It was something to think about.

Chapter 6

Diego watched Kate. She seemed far away, lost in her own thoughts. He hoped she'd be able to contact her family eventually and rid herself of some of the hurt that so clearly weighed on her.

He thought back to the day when he and Jose had realized that their biological parents were trying to get money from them. As lightly as he could talk about it now, and as much as he now understood the difficult situation his parents had been in, that day still hurt to remember. It was still so vivid: the dawning realization about what they really wanted, how Jose shouted at them and ran out the door.

He remembered finding his twin leaning against a wall a couple blocks away, angry and frustrated at the entire world, it seemed. He'd never seen Jose like that before, and at the time he wondered if Jose's carefree demeanor was gone for good. The thought had terrified him.

Diego had tried his best to reassure Jose. Even all these years later, Diego remembered it so clearly, as if it was a movie scene he'd watched over and over…

"We don't need them, Jose. We have a great family already," Diego had told his brother.

Jose's expression didn't change. Diego's heart hurt, just as much for his twin as for himself. Diego was desperate to help him.

"And you know I'll always be here for you, whatever you need. I'm your brother and will have your back no matter what life throws at us, okay? You and me. A team against the world."

Jose gave him a half-hearted smile and the brothers hugged. Then they'd walked back toward the bus that would take them to their loving adoptive parents, who demanded nothing of them and gave them everything they could ever ask for. Two brothers, side by side.

And that was the way it had been ever since. Whatever happened, Diego was ready to protect his brother, be there for him. When Jose fell, Diego was there to pick him up.

And now, instead of *having* Jose's back, he was going to fall for Jose's fiancée and *stab him* in the back? No way.

At least, he wasn't going to act on his feelings. He'd already fallen; he knew that deep down to his bones. The best he could do was hide it. Kate only thought of him as a friend, anyway. They would work together, but otherwise he would stay out of her way.

Starting right now, he thought as he stood. “Is there anything else you need me to do out here?” he asked.

She seemed startled by the abrupt shift, but he held his ground and waited for her answer, hoping she would let him disappear into the house, but also hoping there was something more to work on so he could spend another few minutes in her presence.

“I—I think everything’s done,” she said, seeming to recover herself.

“Good,” he said, nodding. “Enjoy the rest of your day. Since there aren’t any classes today, I’m going to familiarize myself with the school’s paperwork and then catch up on my own work. I’ll probably be busy all day,” he added, fully aware that he would likely be bored out of his mind cramped up in an office for hours.

Still, it was for the best.

He didn’t know what he wished she would say to him, but whatever it was, he didn’t get it. She nodded and said, “I suppose I’ll see you later, then.”

He ignored the part of him that wanted to invent something, anything, for them to do together. “Yes. See you later,” he said. He stayed rooted to the spot for another long moment, his eyes on hers, before he could get himself to walk away.

Damn. Since when did doing the right thing get so hard?

“Wait,” she said.

He turned back to her, equal measures relieved and

frustrated that his escape was stopped. "Does Jose give money to your parents, too?" she asked.

He shouldn't have been surprised that Kate wanted to know about Jose's involvement with their parents; after all, she was marrying him. Still, it broke his heart a little. Diego hid his feelings as best he could and shook his head. "He hasn't gotten over the way they treated us. I hope he will someday," he said.

She nodded, and after a few more moments, he continued on his way toward the house.

After he'd gone no more than twenty yards, he heard running steps behind him. He turned to see Kate jogging his way, trying to catch up. He wasn't sure he could take another question about Jose at the moment, but he waited for her, wondering what she would ask him about her fiancé now.

"I'm starving. Let's get some breakfast at the house before you get to work," she said.

He hadn't expected that, and he quickly ran through possible responses.

I'm not hungry.

I'll grab something and eat it in Pop's office.

I've joined a crazy cult that thinks eating breakfast is a sin.

There were a million ways to avoid sitting down at the table alone with her.

"Okay," he said.

They walked the rest of the way to the house together in silence while Diego tried very hard to convince himself that eating near her wasn't a big deal and really was the only polite thing to do. Plus, he had to eat, right?

Diego was constantly surprised by how little control he had over himself when they were together. He could make himself work hour after hour, staring at spreadsheets and number projections until his eyes burned. On a horse he could outride almost anyone. He was steady, a master of self-control and clear thinking, a rock. Until he found himself a few feet from Kate Andrews. Then he became putty, ready to fall all over himself the moment he looked at her.

No, this wouldn't do. Inside the kitchen, he glanced at the clock. "It's not even seven," he whispered. "And it's Sunday. I don't want to make a big ruckus—"

"You're right. We'll need to cook quietly. You grab the eggs," she whispered back.

He had been about to tell her that he would eat later, once more people were up, show her and himself that he wouldn't be controlled by those feelings he had for her. But then she smiled at him and held a finger to her lips as if they were coconspirators, and there was no way he could argue with that. Everyone had their weakness, and unfortunately his weakness had reddish hair, deep green eyes and a mischievous smile.

So he went to the fridge and pulled out a carton of eggs and some bacon while she opened the bread box and pulled out English muffins. "Breakfast sandwiches sound good?" Kate asked.

They sounded great, so the two of them got to work frying the eggs and bacon, toasting the muffins and making coffee. In just a few minutes they sat at the kitchen table, two steaming mugs and plates with a couple sandwiches each.

Diego took his first bite and leaned back a little, enjoying the sensation. It had been a long time since he'd risen before the rooster and really earned his breakfast. For months he'd done nothing but talk to clients, answer emails and fill out spreadsheets, nothing like the honest day's work he'd gotten in this morning. It felt great.

He wanted nothing more than to saddle a horse and go for a ride around the property and beyond, feeling the hot summer wind blowing in his face, the animal beneath him pounding the earth with its hooves.

With Kate racing along beside him.

Diego shook himself out of his fantasy and let reality crash back down. He had work to do inside, and riding around with Kate during one of the few times they didn't need to be together would just make things harder on himself. No, he needed to pull himself together and get his mind where it belonged—adding numbers and reading forms.

"Ugh," he grunted.

"Is there something wrong with the food?" Kate asked, looking worried.

Diego hadn't realized he'd made the noise out loud. Now she was looking at him, waiting to hear why he had sounded like he was being forced to eat liver. Or that Jell-O thing his mom had made the day before.

"No, nothing. I was just thinking about all the paperwork I have to do," he confessed.

She wrinkled her nose at the idea. "*Ugh* is right," she said.

"Paperwork isn't your thing?" he said, trying to be politely curious and nothing more.

"Definitely not. I'm glad Pop is happy to take care of it all. I'd rather be out in the sunshine than stuck behind a desk," she told him.

"Me, too," he said, thinking of the image he'd conjured up before. The two of them riding around the property together, the horses' hooves kicking up dust.

"Isn't your job right now mostly just that?" she asked.

Diego had gotten so sucked into the picture in his mind that he had lost the thread of the conversation. "Just what?"

"Just paperwork. From what Jose has told me about it, he goes around and checks out stock while you figure out prices and costs and transportation, that sort of thing. So don't you spend pretty much all your time doing that behind a desk?" She looked at him, curious and concerned.

Diego didn't know what to say. She was right; he was always inside and he hated it. He was a cowboy through and through. Life was just better on a horse. "I'm good at it," he said, but that didn't seem to be enough of an answer. "And it needs to happen or the business will fail," Diego added finally.

Kate raised an eyebrow at him. "Would failing be the worst thing in the world? Maybe then you could do something you enjoy instead."

Diego stood. This was getting too close to some difficult truths for his comfort. "I need to get busy," he said as he picked up his plate. "I'll eat the rest in the office. Thank you for the meal."

She nodded, her emerald eyes piercing into his, seeing more than he wanted her to. Finally he turned away and left the room.

In the little office, he set down the plate on one of the piles of papers that covered the desk. He stared at it for a minute, his thoughts wandering back to Kate's words. He wasn't very hungry anymore.

With a sigh, he sat down in the chair, pulled himself up to the desk and began sifting through the paperwork for the riding school that littered the surface. He had plenty of his own work—calls to make, stock spreadsheets to update—but just now that sounded about as appealing as chewing rocks, so he convinced himself that he needed to prepare for the first classes by understanding all the financials and everything else involved in running Pop's school. He knew he was stalling and he could even lose out on some stock transactions if he didn't get to them soon, but the thought of it was too much at the moment.

Besides, the office was a mess, and he couldn't possibly be expected to get anything done until it was cleaned up. Apparently Pop's organizational style was less organizational and more set-it-and-forget-it.

He scooped together all the papers that appeared to be student documents before going through each one to ensure it was filled out fully. Then he filed everything carefully into some empty folders he found in a stack on the floor; they were evidently the result of another of Pop's dollar-store runs, probably with the intent of a tidying spree that never happened. Once Diego finished with one stack of papers, he moved on to the next pile, then the next, then the next.

By the time he finished sorting through everything, the desk was clear, but his mind was a jumble of questions. It was obvious that he needed to speak to Pop.

Diego left the office in search of him, and found Jose, Ma and Pop in the kitchen eating breakfast together. Diego sat down and looked at his adoptive father. "Pop, I've been going through the financials for the riding school, and I've noticed that some of the kids are paying next to nothing for their classes. The amount you're bringing in can't possibly be enough to pay Kate, feed and care for the horses, *and* give you any sort of an income."

Diego was sincerely worried. Had Pop started going a little senile and not realized he was charging way too little? Were his parents in financial trouble?

Pop shrugged. "People pay what they can pay. The riding school has never made money."

Diego furrowed his brow. "How can you pay your own expenses?"

Jose eyed Ma and Pop. "Don't expect to come live with me if you two lose the house. I run a tight ship at my place and don't need any jokesters like you around," he said, pointing at the elderly couple with a smirk.

Pop sighed and set down his fork before looking at his twin sons, who were both staring at him. "I guess you two are old enough to know by now that the riding school isn't the only form of income around here."

"Ooh, mysterious cash flow!" Jose exclaimed, rubbing his hands together. "Is it illegal? Please tell me it's illegal."

Diego and Ma, who were sitting on either side of

Jose, smacked him on each arm in unison before turning back to Pop.

"Ma and I own some more property out of town a ways and we had a company interested in looking for oil on it before you two were even born. And they found oil. So we have enough to get by," Pop said.

Jose and Diego looked at each other, clearly wondering the same thing. Diego decided it would be too impolite to ask.

But Jose didn't have the same qualms. "Are we millionaires?"

Pop raised an eyebrow at Jose. "Ma and I have plenty to hold us over for the rest of our lives and leave a little something for our children. The rest goes to those less fortunate. Now, I expect you two to go about your lives just the same as you would otherwise. Don't be expecting some big windfall when we're gone or you'll be sorely disappointed."

Diego smiled at his adoptive father. He would expect nothing less from the people who'd raised him. "I'd prefer to have you two around a good long while, anyway," he told them.

The couple looked at Diego with smiles, and the three of them shared a moment of understanding.

"You heard them, Diego," Jose said, standing and breaking into the silence. "We aren't going to be millionaires unless we do it ourselves. That's why we need to get our business going. Then we can be rich, too, like these folks apparently have been our entire lives, despite never letting me get the good cereal when I was a kid," Jose said, giving Ma a look of disappointment.

"That stuff rots your teeth, Jose," Ma told him, just as she had hundreds of times before.

Jose shook his head, clearly reliving the difficulties of his childhood, before turning back to Diego. "So just let me know what rancher I need to finesse next," he said before sticking a last forkful of egg into his mouth and taking his plate to the sink.

Diego nodded and stood up wearily. It was time to get to his actual work.

Kate walked Queen Bee back into the barn under the hot noonday sun, despite the horse's reluctance to leave the paddock. "I told you," Kate explained to the stubborn mare, "I'm not putting you in your stall. We're going to go for a ride. You love going out for a ride."

The mare seemed to prefer lazing in the paddock, and she told Kate so with a snort and shake of her head. "I need to get some air and distance. Be a pal, okay?" Kate cajoled, giving the horse a handful of oats as soon as they crossed the threshold of the barn.

Queen Bee nuzzled Kate's palm until every last bit was gone, suddenly in a much more amenable mood. Kate gave her a pat and looped the lead over a post before going to get a saddle.

After Diego's abrupt disappearance from the breakfast table, she had tried to relax and read a bit, but her brain was too full to let her do anything so sedentary. She had too much to think about, from the possibility of contacting her parents to why Diego was working on a business he didn't enjoy. Not to mention her feelings for Diego and coming up with a plan that might free her from what her mind had dubbed quote-unquote The Ring Problem, while also allowing her to still work here.

Did she even *want* to work here now that Pop had turned it over to Diego? Was the situation permanent or temporary? And her feelings, were they temporary? She didn't have an answer for any of those questions.

And she certainly didn't want to sit down for lunch with Diego, Jose and their parents while she tried to sort them out. So instead she was going to go for a long hot ride. Hopefully by the time she was done, she wouldn't feel quite so off-balance.

Kate cinched the saddle belt on Queen Bee and made sure everything was tight and secure. "You ready, girl?" she asked.

The horse turned her ears toward the open barn door, as if she was listening to something, and Kate focused her attention in that direction. From where she stood, she could see the large ranch house she'd thought of as home for the past few months. A tall man stepped out the back door as she watched, and for a heart-thumping moment she thought Diego was coming out to the barn. She wondered if he was looking for her.

The feeling quickly turned to disappointment, however, as she recognized Jose's saunter. If it hadn't been obvious before, her reaction made Kate absolutely positive that she needed to break off her engagement with Jose as soon as she could come up with the kindest way to say it. Even if things never happened between her and Diego—

Which they obviously never could, she reminded herself angrily.

Regardless, she and Jose didn't work and never would, and keeping the engagement going would be wrong. How could she let him down easy? There *had* to be a way, right?

"Wait here, girl," she told Queen Bee, who looked displeased to be saddled and then left waiting. "I'll bring you more oats to make it up to you," Kate promised.

The mare just snorted as Kate walked toward the barn door to see where Jose was going. If she knew where he was, she could sort out some thoughts. Then she would catch up to him and

Apparently he'd been heading to the barn all along, because he was suddenly standing in the doorway, just a few feet from her.

Kate was so surprised by his sudden appearance that she jumped back, but he didn't seem to notice.

"Hey!" he said, giving her his most endearing smile and walking toward her. "I need to leave for a few days. Big work thing Diego can't do since he's the head honcho around here now. I'll miss you."

"Okay, but I—" she began.

He cut her off with a quick kiss. "Can't talk now. Gotta run. Text me and I'll get back to you in the next day or so."

With that he was leaving the barn, practically jogging in his hurry.

He was leaving, and she hadn't said anything. The ring would sit on her nightstand indefinitely until it wound up on her finger and she was getting married to Jose and—

"I don't want to marry you," she blurted out, almost at a shout, just as he exited the barn door.

Darn. That was definitely not the way she had wanted to go about it.

Jose stopped midstride and turned around, looking confused, as if he'd heard her wrong. She took a deep breath and tried to come up with something to say, cursing herself for her mind's utter blankness. "Listen, Jose, I think you're great," she began, already hating where she was headed.

"You don't want to marry me?" he asked, as if this idea was complete and utter nonsense.

Kate shook her head, knowing there was nothing she could say to fix this. "I'm sorry," she added quietly.

There was a long silence while she waited for him to process what she'd said. Finally he gave her a smile that looked forced and not a bit genuine. "You're not the first girl to think I'm not marriage material," he said with a shrug.

"Jose—" she began, wanting to comfort him or stand up for herself, she wasn't sure which.

But before she could figure out what to say, he gestured in the direction of his truck. "I'd love to stay and continue this incredibly awkward discussion, but I need to go."

With that he turned on his heel and left, and she was alone in the barn once more. She couldn't even begin to think of how those two minutes had just changed everything about her life. Suddenly she was single, and possibly jobless and homeless. Jose making jokes didn't reassure her that he was okay with what had just happened; he was the kind of guy that would make jokes at a funeral. He could be totally devastated and still have something comical to say.

Kate sighed. Grabbing another handful of oats, she walked back to Queen Bee, who was watching her intently. "See, that wasn't so bad, was it?" she asked sarcastically as the horse munched. There was nothing she could do—or wanted to do—at the moment, except hop on the horse and get as far away from people as possible.

"Let's go make some dust, QB," Kate said, wiping her hands on her jeans before pulling herself up into the saddle. She grabbed the reins and took a deep breath. It was time to ride.

Diego leaned back in his chair and stretched. He hadn't gotten much done, but he was exhausted and hungry. The breakfast sandwich, which no longer sat on a pile of miscellaneous papers, had been wilting for the past few hours. It looked sad and unappetizing, and the leftovers in the fridge were calling to him. Work could wait.

With a heave, Diego unfolded his long frame from behind the desk and left the office. He found Ma, Pop and Jose in the kitchen once again, but this time they weren't eating. Ma and Pop looked concerned, and Jose's smile didn't reach his eyes. Diego wondered what could possibly have happened to cause this sort of reaction.

"I'm going to head out for a while," Jose told Ma,

who looked even more upset now that her son was leaving so suddenly.

"Please don't feel like you need to leave, dear," Ma insisted, but before she could implore further, Jose nodded toward Diego, who was still standing in the doorway watching the proceedings.

"I was going to head out, anyway. Cattle to buy and all that," Jose said, as if Diego had given him some sort of assignment.

Diego stared at Jose. What cattle could he possibly be talking about? Diego wasn't sending him anywhere, so he was obviously lying about that. And why were they all acting so strange?

Diego followed Jose as he grabbed his hat and boots from the entryway and walked out the door. Diego wanted answers.

Jose sat down on the porch to pull on his boots. Diego sat next to him and waited to hear what could possibly be happening that would cause Ma to look at Jose like that. To make him lie to their parents. Jose gave Diego a grin that made Diego wary. It was Jose's the world-is-against-me smile.

"Do you remember Adrianne?"

Diego thought for a minute. "Your girlfriend from high school?" Diego asked, not sure where Jose was going with this.

"Yeah, well, funnily enough," he said with a big exhale, "she called me up and said she'd like to do a paternity test."

Diego was confused. "You're helping her find her father?"

Jose rolled his eyes at his brother. "Come on, Diego," he said.

"Oh," Diego said, finally catching on.

"Yeah. She and I saw each other again a couple years back and, well, the chemistry was still there. Let's put it that way."

"Then why didn't you two get back together?" Diego asked. He remembered how crazy Jose had been for Adrianne and how broken up he'd been, in his own Jose way, when she'd moved away for college. They'd even tried long-distance for a while, but it hadn't worked out.

Jose stretched out his legs, his bootheels rapping against the wooden boards of the porch. "She said that I was too immature, can you believe that?"

"So you what, had a one-night-stand and now she has a little kid that might be yours?"

"Pretty much," Jose said. "She's not sure. Apparently there's more to the story than what I know."

"And that's why Ma looked so upset?" Diego asked, a little confused.

"No, she doesn't know about that. She's upset because Kate just broke up with me."

Diego felt like the air had gone out of his lungs. "What? She broke up with you because of a kid?"

That was so unlike Kate. Or at least what he thought he knew about Kate.

Jose didn't look at Diego, just shook his head. "Didn't even tell her about it. She doesn't want to marry me, I guess. Apparently I'm a good guy, though. So I've got that going for me," he finished with a false levity that Diego could see right through.

Diego wanted to console his brother, but what could he say? *I'm sorry the woman I like doesn't want to be with you?* Diego felt wracked with guilt. Even though he knew Kate didn't feel the same way and her decision to end things with Jose had nothing to do with him, Diego still felt like a traitor.

Before Diego could figure out what to say, Jose stood up and walked to his truck without another word. Or another joke.

Diego's heart ached for his brother.

Jose gave him a little wave and climbed into his car.

No, Diego couldn't let his brother leave like this. He had to do the right thing, even though he wasn't sure exactly what that was. He jogged over to the truck, even though he was still in his socks. "Jose—" he began.

Jose looked at him, and words failed Diego. He couldn't do anything to hurt his brother more right now. He would confess another day, when the wound wasn't so fresh. For the moment, Jose just needed a friend, a brother. Diego could do that much. "If you need anything, you let me know, okay? Whatever happens with Adrianne and the kid, I'm here for you," Diego said at last.

Jose rolled his eyes. "This isn't an afternoon special, Diego," he said.

But then Jose threw him a half grin and Diego knew his brother appreciated what he'd said.

Diego stepped away from the truck as Jose put it into gear and drove away.

Diego walked back to the steps and sat down, trying to wrap his mind around everything that had just happened. Things had been moving too quickly the past couple days for his brain to keep up.

Diego walked back into the house to find Ma waiting for him, looking concerned. "Jose's going to be okay," he reassured them.

Ma gave him an irritated look. "I'm not worried about Jose. He'll find someone more suited to him and be just fine, mark my words. They weren't right for each other. You know that as well as I do," she said.

He did. Kate needed someone…

Well, someone like Diego.

Diego banished that thought the moment it appeared and focused his attention back on Ma. Why didn't she ever say something? Kate would've listened to her. Before he could ask, Ma gave him a look that told him she knew exactly what he was thinking. "It's not my place to tell you kids what to do. Each of you needs to make your own choices and mistakes."

Before Diego could point out plenty of times that she had chosen to meddle into their lives for their own good, Ma turned the conversation back to her purpose.

"I'm worried that Kate will think she needs to leave because of all this. You have to go and make sure she's staying. Convince her that we all need her here, won't you?" she asked.

Diego nodded as he swallowed a sigh. Kate was a valuable member of the ranch and he didn't want her to feel forced to pick up and move, but it left him in a tough spot.

Now Kate was single, and he couldn't do anything about it. Neither could he avoid her. He felt trapped.

Ma gave him a little smile. "I tell you, son, it does my heart good knowing the riding school is in the hands of you two. I'm sure it'll do you both good to work with each other. I think you will be two peas in a pod before you know it," she said, patting Diego on the arm before leading him toward the back door. "Get going, now. Time's a-wasting, and I'm sure Kate could use a friend as well as a little reassurance."

Before he knew it, Diego was being shoved outside, his boots under his arm, where Ma tucked them before she popped his hat on his head and closed the door. Diego wasn't completely sure what had just happened, but there was no choice but to follow Ma's orders. He slipped into his cowboy boots, resettled his hat on his head and went off in search of Kate.

She wasn't in the barn, but the empty spot where her saddle should have been clued him in to what she was up to.

When he wanted to think, he liked to get on a horse and ride. He would bet good money that Kate did, too.

He saddled up Sammy, an easygoing gelding who happily chomped on oats as Diego cinched the belt tight. Then he set off toward the copse of trees that ran along the southern edge of their land. It was just a guess, but with the stifling July heat and blazing sun, it seemed unlikely she'd be anywhere unshaded.

After a few minutes of trotting, Sammy and Diego broke into the cover of the trees and breathed in the cooler air. Diego looked around. It wasn't a giant forest or anything, but the woods had several riding trails and finding Kate could prove difficult if she'd been wandering for a while.

So he did the only thing he couid think of—he shouted, "Marco!"

There was silence for a few seconds before he heard a faint "Polo!" off to his left.

Diego turned that direction and started wandering along. Sure enough, it only took a minute riding along the trail to find Queen Bee grazing and Kate sitting on a rock, breaking a twig into pieces. "Marco Polo? That's how you find someone in the woods?" she asked him.

Diego gave her a little grin. "I've been through some pretty rigorous wilderness training. It's in all the survival guides."

Kate chuckled. "I think because Jose is such a joker, people forget that you're funny, too." There was an awkward moment before she said, "You heard what happened between Jose and me, huh?"

Diego nodded. He chose his words carefully so he wouldn't betray himself or Jose. "Ma was worried you were thinking about leaving. She wanted you to know that your job here is yours as long as you want it."

Kate watched him from where she sat, tossing the twig pieces one by one onto the ground. She was suddenly very serious. "What about you? Do you want me around, even after everything?"

Diego didn't know how to answer that. *No, and also more than anything.* "You are great at your job. The riding school needs you," he said. "I have no hard feelings about your decision to end the engagement."

Lord, was that the truth. Unfortunately, he couldn't

explain his real reason for it, that he wouldn't have been able to bear watching her walk down the aisle toward his brother instead of him.

Those weren't words he could say, so he bit his tongue. They watched each other for a few seconds, and Diego wondered what Kate was thinking. Then she stood up. "We're going to take a few of the classes along this trail next week. We should check it out and be sure it's safe," Kate told him as she swung into her saddle.

Diego didn't even attempt to argue with himself that he should try to get out of it. When Kate was settled into her saddle, they continued along the trail, side by side, even though it wasn't really wide enough for two horses.

"We weren't really engaged, you know," Kate said after a few minutes of riding silently.

"What?" Diego asked, confused.

"I never said yes. He sprung it on me in such a public setting and it was all so awkward that I didn't know how to say no, but I never said yes, and I just couldn't find the right time to talk to him about it until today," she explained.

"Oh," Diego responded, for lack of anything better to say.

Honestly, he didn't know what to think about that. It made so much more sense than Kate agreeing to marriage and then backing out a couple days later. But it didn't really change anything for him, or for Jose.

"I just thought you should know," she added, looking a little uncomfortable.

After a brief silence, Diego decided it was best to change the subject. "Any particular reason you chose to ride Queen Bee?" he asked, looking over at the horse that some would call regal, but most would call stubborn and difficult.

Kate patted the horse on the neck affectionately. "She's wonderful," Kate said. "I think she's the smartest horse on the ranch. When you talk to her, it's like she's really listening."

Diego wondered what secrets Queen Bee knew about Kate.

"Now, Sammy," she continued, gesturing to Diego's horse. "He's content to follow directions his whole life and do exactly what people expect him to."

"You say that like it's a bad thing," Diego said.

Kate shrugged. "I appreciate the kind of character it takes to stand up to others and let people know what you want," she said.

Diego wasn't sure they were still talking about horses.

Luckily, he didn't need to respond because they came across a downed tree blocking part of the trail. Without saying a word, they simultaneously jumped out of their saddles and looped their reins over nearby tree branches.

With a big heave, they shoved and pushed until the trail was clear.

Diego couldn't help but smile at Kate when they had finished the task, and she smiled back. To work together so seamlessly, like a team, felt good. Really good.

Too good.

The grin faded from his face and he turned back to Sammy. "I should probably get back to the house," he said.

"Oh. Okay," Kate responded, sounding disappointed. "I'll finish looking over the trail."

Diego almost wavered, but he had been walking into dangerous territory yet again, and if he didn't get away now, he wasn't sure he'd be able to control himself. So he hopped onto Sammy without looking at her and turned back toward the ranch. Before he could leave Kate, though, he needed to know one thing: "So you're staying on at the riding school, right?" he asked.

He told himself it was better if she decided to leave, but as the moments dragged on without an answer, Diego began to feel dread course through him. What if he never got to see her again? He looked into her eyes and she stared back. He was captivated by their green depths, just as he always was.

Finally, she spoke. "I'm not going anywhere," she told him, her voice firm and sure.

Relief flooded his body. She was staying. Outwardly, all he did was nod, give her a small smile and urge Sammy along the trail, back the way they had come.

He knew he shouldn't be happy that she wanted to stick around the ranch, but he couldn't help it. As hard as it was to be around her, he knew that having her completely out of his life would be so much worse.

After brushing down Sammy and getting him settled in a stall, Diego trudged back up to the house. It wasn't even suppertime yet, but he was exhausted.

The moment he stepped through the back door, Ma was peppering him with questions. "What took you so long, dear? You convinced Kate to stay on here, didn't you? Was she worried? What happened? Why aren't you talking?"

Diego knew if he pointed out that she hadn't yet given him a chance to talk, he'd earn himself a smack on the arm for being impertinent, so he ignored the last question. "She's going to stay. I had to go find her out by the stream, and then we checked the trail for hazards so we can take a class along there soon."

Ma gave him a look of approval, then gave a glance out the window. "Well, where is she, then?"

"Still out on the trail," he said.

Ma scowled. "You left her out there alone?" she asked, sounding incredulous.

Diego didn't mention that she'd been angry at him for being gone too long thirty seconds before. "She's smart and strong enough to handle anything out there, Ma," he retorted.

Her independence was one of the many things he loved about Kate.

Appreciated, he amended. *Not loved.*

His heart disagreed, but he tried to ignore it as Ma bustled around him. "Well, I suppose so. And I imagine you're starving, though supper isn't for a good while yet," she said as she set a plate of leftovers on the table and steered him to it.

Diego sat and started to eat, though his appetite had disappeared somewhere in the chaos of the day.

"I tell you," Ma continued. "I think a few days away and Jose will be right as rain. I sure am glad you had a job for him today."

Diego felt guilty. Even though it wasn't his lie, saying nothing still felt wrong. But where Jose had gone wasn't Diego's secret to tell.

Diego had strived his entire life to be an honorable person. He didn't like to lie or keep secrets, and now he was keeping more than he could handle. He was holding back truths from Kate and Jose and Ma and even himself. Because if he was honest to himself about how much he liked Kate, that he had fallen completely in love with her, it would just hurt more to be so close and so far away from what he wanted.

Because out of all those people, he was honor-bound to do right by his brother. The hope of possibility that had quietly built inside him ever since Jose had told them about the broken engagement was hard to stifle, but Diego knew one fact: he couldn't pursue Jose's ex and risk hurting his brother more.

Diego took another bite of his meal, feeling tired and careworn. He'd had enough of this day to fill a lifetime.

Chapter 7

Kate rose even earlier the next morning than she had the one before, practically jumping out of bed. She sneaked down the stairs in the half light, careful not to wake those that were still sleeping.

The one person she wanted to see was already awake, she hoped.

Her stomach jumped when she stepped into the lighted barn and found Diego already brushing one of the mares. She was glad to see him, and not just for his capable horse-grooming skills.

The day before, when they spoke out in the woods, Kate had made a decision: she couldn't pretend she didn't like Diego, and she wanted to explore those feelings. Not right away, of course, but she couldn't just accept that her past with Jose meant she'd never be able to have a future with Diego, even though it felt so right.

"Good morning," she said, smiling at his back.

"Morning," he replied, not even turning his head.

She stopped and watched him. From the jerky way he was moving the brush across the animal's back, it was clear to her that something was wrong. Kate wanted to go up to him and touch his shoulder, perhaps give him a hug. Instead, she grabbed a brush and moved to sweep it over the horse's neck. "Not able to sleep in, huh?" she asked, trying to get a good look at his face.

Diego shook his head but remained silent. By the circles under his eyes, she wasn't sure if he'd slept at all. She wanted to pry. Was this all because of her and Jose, or was there something else wrong? She knew she shouldn't ask, though, so she changed the topic instead.

"I spent some time yesterday thinking about what you said," she told him as she moved on to another horse.

"About talking to your parents?" he asked, seeming to jolt out of his bad mood a little.

"Yeah," Kate said. "I took your advice and reached out to my mom yesterday. I can't promise it'll go any further than a phone call, but I'm glad I took that step."

She didn't add that part of the reason she'd done it was because she'd been feeling so worried she might lose her surrogate family that it convinced her to connect with her real one.

"That's wonderful, Kate. And brave," Diego said in such a sincere tone that it went straight to her heart.

She almost said something then, told him how she

felt about him, but stopped herself. It was too soon. Kate knew that. If she wanted them to have a chance, she needed to go slow, despite what her heart and body desired.

"Find anything interesting in all your paperwork yesterday?" she asked. She knew she was prying a little bit now, trying to discover reasons for his mood that didn't have to do with his twin, but she figured that question was safe enough.

Diego shrugged. "Just that Pop is a big softy, but I already knew that."

Kate smiled to herself. "He really is, and I kind of love that about him," she said.

"Me, too," he answered.

Kate tried to think of what else to say. Part of her wanted to ask him if he was *sure* he was okay with her staying on at the ranch, but part of her was scared to hear the answer. She was sure he had feelings for her, but...

But what if he didn't?

Or what if he did, but her past with Jose was a deal-breaker forever?

Neither of those thoughts were very pleasant, so she felt relief when Diego interrupted them.

"We should probably get to the real work," he said, putting down his brush.

Kate followed suit, and soon they were mucking out the stalls together. This time they mucked out one stall at a time instead of separating. Kate reveled in the closeness despite her worries and her vow to take things slow. She couldn't help that every time she was near Diego, she felt more excited, like the air around her was charged with electricity. She also felt soothed and relaxed, as if this was where she was meant to be.

Despite their proximity, they completed nearly all the morning tasks before either one said anything more than a word or two. She was just starting to think that she would need to say something when he broke the silence for her.

"So what cold city are you from?" he asked.

That wasn't a topic she'd expected. "How did you know I'm from a cold city?" she asked, curious where he'd gotten that information. She didn't talk about her hometown much and doubted even Jose had any idea where she'd grown up. Then again, Jose didn't pay attention like Diego did.

"Yesterday you said you had gotten on a bus and left behind snow, cities and disappointing families. So I wondered what cold city you lived in."

Kate was impressed. She knew he was thoughtful, but it was hard to believe that he'd been listening closely enough to pick up on little details like that. She would need to watch herself around him or she might accidentally confess something she didn't want to say quite yet.

"My mom lived in Chicago, my dad in Duluth," she said.

"No wonder you left," Diego commented with a shake of his head, earning a chuckle from her.

"Seriously. Even if they were the best parents, I would hate it there. As it was…well, leaving was really the best choice for me."

He nodded but didn't say anything else. Kate didn't want to let the quiet engulf them again, and she racked her brain trying to come up with a topic of conversation. Something light. Something anyone could talk about without bringing up awkward family issues or that tingly feeling she got when she was close to him. Something that wouldn't embarrass her.

"Books!" she decided in triumph.

"Books?" Diego asked, looking confused.

Kate blushed, in disbelief that she'd really just shouted the word *books* aloud. So much for not embarrassing herself.

"Um, I meant… Do you read books?"

It came out sounding like she thought he was an idiot. Apparently she was totally incapable of speaking to Diego like a normal human being right now.

Kate was really starting to hate herself a little bit. Even if they managed to talk about books, she knew he would probably roll his eyes at her current reading material. She didn't look at him, hoping this would be over soon so they could go back to awkward silence.

Diego just laughed, and his mood seemed instantly better. "Yes, I read books sometimes. Do you read books?"

Kate accepted that this conversation was going to crash and burn, but at least it seemed like it made his day a bit better. Might as well not fight it. "Yes, I read books sometimes, too," she answered.

He turned back to the stall and started shoveling again. Kate did, too, relieved to move past the whole situation and let that terrible conversation die. Maybe if she never spoke around him again, she could avoid sounding any more like a fool than she already had.

"Read anything good lately?" he asked without looking up from his task.

She gave her shovelful of manure a wry smile. *Here we go,* she thought. Why did she start this topic? "I've been reading *Eat, Pray, Love*," she said, waiting for the derision every male seemed to have toward that book.

"That one surprised me. I liked it way more than I thought I would," he said.

She glanced over at him, her eyebrows knitted. "You've *read* it?" she asked, shocked.

Diego shrugged. "Yeah, a couple years ago. Amy was in Bali at the time, read it and told me she liked it, so I grabbed a copy."

How many times could this guy surprise her? How many times would everything about him shout "I'm not like anybody you've met! I'm so much better!" straight at her heart?

Diego was so comfortable with himself, he'd not only read *Eat, Pray, Love*, but he'd also admitted it.

After they discussed the travels and adventures of Elizabeth Gilbert, the conversation died down again. This time, the silence didn't feel awkward and Diego seemed happy, but Kate still didn't want silence. She wanted to hear what Diego had to say about literature, life… Anything, really.

Diego's constant lack of judgment made her feel free to be herself, and she wanted as much of that as she could get. Even more, he was intelligent and insightful, and she liked listening to what he had to say. When he spoke, his voice washed over her in a way she couldn't describe, except that it was wonderful.

"What's the most recent book you've read?" she asked.

"Well, most recently I read *Click, Clack, Moo*," he answered, completely serious.

"What?" she asked, looking over at him. Surely she'd misheard.

"Click, Clack, Moo: Cows That Type," he clarified.

But things were no more clear on her end, so she just kept staring at him, waiting for more as she tried to hide her smile.

"I was picking out some books as a gift for Amy's baby. It's not bad, as far as baby books go."

"Interesting plot?" she asked with a laugh.

He grinned back at her and nodded. "Surprisingly good, yes. Fewer exotic locations than *Eat, Pray, Love*, unfortunately."

And they were off again, discussing the finer points of a book written for children. Meanwhile they finished the work on the stalls. The barn was ready for the day.

"Breakfast?" Kate asked, feeling her stomach rumble.

"Breakfast," Diego agreed.

The two of them left the barn together. The sun was up by this time, and the heat of the day had already begun to build. Kate looked at the time. "The first group will be getting here in an hour or so. There will be lessons until noon. Normally I would spend the hours after lunch cleaning the barn, so I'm not sure what I'll do then. Maybe I'll need to pick up a copy of *Click, Clack, Moo*."

Diego chuckled as they entered the kitchen, where

Ma was attempting to make breakfast. *Attempting* was the best word for it because Pop was trying to help, but with his cast and crutch, he was more a hindrance than anything else. Still, Kate could see that Ma didn't have the heart to tell the injured man to go sit down.

"Hey, Pop," Kate said, giving Ma an understanding glance. "Would you mind sitting with me for a few minutes? I'd like to discuss today's groups with you."

Pop looked up. "Can it wait until breakfast is on the table? I need to finish chopping these tomatoes," he said as one of his crutches slipped and hit Ma in the hip. "Sorry, dear," he told her.

"I'll take over here. You go talk to Kate," Diego said.

In a few seconds the two of them had Pop in a chair with Kate beside him and Diego helping Ma, who looked very grateful to no longer be in danger of falling crutches.

Kate was happy to chat about the students and lessons with Pop while the others made the meal. He loved the riding school as much as she did, if that was possible, and his enthusiasm made her smile. She knew it was hard for him not to be out there on a horse, but he seemed to accept that until the cast was off he would be doing no such thing. Kate could see that having Diego there did a lot to appease the old man, and to Kate that spoke volumes about Diego's capabilities.

After breakfast, Diego and Kate stood in unison. "Should we get the horses saddled?" Diego asked her.

Kate nodded. "We have a pretty big group this morning. Eight students—"

"Under the age of ten. I'm guessing you normally

saddle up Irene, Sandy, Ricardo and Jessie for this group?"

Pop chuckled. "I told you he'd do a fine job, didn't I, Kate?"

Kate had to agree.

Ma crossed her arms, a big smile on her face. "I was sure as could be that you two would keep our students learning. Now get out there and teach those young'uns a thing or two about riding horses," she said, ushering them out of the kitchen.

Kate followed Diego to the door, where he opened it and stepped aside to allow her to pass through first. It was a small thing, but the act made her foolish heart flop in her chest, and the smell of him as she passed by was enough to make the blood rush to her cheeks as it pounded through her veins.

"Good boy." She heard Ma mutter the two words under her breath, but it sounded more like she was talking to herself than Diego, so Kate dismissed it as a mother's approval of her son's chivalry.

Diego and Kate walked together toward the barn. "Cassie's twins are in this class, right? They seem to have learned quickly how to fit in down here in Texas. We're a long way from Minneapolis," Diego said.

Kate was happy to have something to focus on besides how close his arm was to hers as they walked side by side. "They're good little riders for their age," she agreed.

They entered the barn and started saddling horses, working quickly. It was obvious Diego was as practiced at it as she was.

"Amy's daughter will probably be an ace rider, with the parents she has," Diego said over Sandy's back. "Did you know Amy was in the junior rodeo circuit for a time?"

Kate nodded. "I've seen her trophies," she said as she checked one saddle before moving on to the next.

Diego coughed, as if he'd choked on his own breath, and she knew why. She had been sleeping in Amy's room the past few nights, and that was where she'd noticed the trophies. That was also where he'd meant to sleep when they had wound up kissing each other. The kiss that had sent her spiraling into so many feelings for him she didn't know what to do with herself when they were just walking near one another.

She desperately pulled the topic back into safe territory.

"I can't believe Amy's little girl will be born any day now," Kate said.

"Yeah. It's weird to think of her as a mom, but she'll be great at it," Diego replied.

Kate agreed. She had watched Amy for almost the entire pregnancy, and she had never seen a woman more caring and loving toward her unborn child.

There was nothing that showed the passage of Kate's time on the ranch more than Amy's pregnancy. When Kate had first moved to Spring Valley, Amy wasn't even showing. Now she had a beach-ball-sized stomach. Kate had even felt the baby kicking, one of the stranger experiences in her life.

Kate unconsciously touched her own stomach as she thought how strange it must feel from the inside.

Then she dropped her hand to her side, holding back a sigh, and got back to work. She had always wanted kids of her own, and watching Amy as she anticipated her baby's arrival was both exciting and a sad reminder of how far she was from that part of life.

She was single again, starting over. And if things didn't work out the way she hoped with Diego…

She glanced over at Diego, then away, wondering how long it could take her to move on from her feelings and fall for somebody new. The answer was disheartening.

And if she messed things up because of those feelings, she would probably need to move away and wouldn't even be able to live vicariously through Amy, and watch her little one transform from a newborn into a baby, then a toddler, then…

But it *could* work—she was sure of it. If she was just patient.

"Everything okay?" Diego asked, his voice full of concern.

Kate had so many conflicting emotions that she didn't know how to answer, but a car door slamming nearby caught her attention. The first of the day's students was arriving.

"You should go introduce yourself to the kids. I'll bring the horses to the paddock," she said as she gathered the leads of the saddled and ready horses.

He looked as if he might not accept her avoidance of the question, but she turned and began walking away with the horses, not looking back until she heard the murmur of voices as Diego spoke with whomever had arrived so far.

Kate looked over to see how the introductions were going. Her jaw dropped at what she saw: Marian, one of their shyest little girls, didn't have her arms wrapped around her father, as was usually the case, but instead had them tightly clutched around Diego's neck as he kneeled beside her. She was hugging him with all her might.

Marian's parents beamed down as Diego laughed, and after another minute of conversation they were gone without their daughter shedding a single tear. In fact, she was so absorbed in whatever she was saying to Diego that she hardly noticed their goodbyes.

Soon more of the six-to-eight-year-old group had arrived, and Kate watched the parents and children greet Diego with as much enthusiasm as Marian did. Even the older siblings of the students gave Diego a hug, a high five or, on one occasion, a very intricate and involved secret handshake that left everyone giggling.

Kate stood beside the paddock where the children would be riding that day, completely mystified about what was going on. In all the time she'd been there, Diego had never been around long enough to make this kind of connection with all these children, yet they were greeting him like a best friend.

All except the DelRio family, who had moved to Spring Valley in March, though it only took a few seconds before Isaac DelRio was grinning as widely as everyone else.

In just a few minutes, everyone had arrived and the

entire class was gathered around Diego. She could hear the sound of him speaking but couldn't make out any of the words. His voice was a soft rumble in her ear, both enticing and soothing. She found herself getting lost in it.

When all the students turned toward the paddock and started running with all their might, she was so shocked that she burst out laughing.

Diego, who was still sitting on his haunches even though the group of children was gone, gave her a big grin. She found herself smiling back as the kids crossed the grassy expanse between them.

Reluctantly, Kate turned her attention to the kids as they began screeching to a halt next to the paddock. After saying her hellos, she gestured at the animals behind her. "Today we're going to practice turning and start learning the basics of barrel racing. I know some of you," she said, eyeing two boys, "want to start flying around those curves immediately, but we need to learn the right technique first so nobody gets hurt. Not you, not the horse. Everybody ready?" Kate asked.

Eight heads bobbed in unison. Diego walked up beside her and they all turned to him as if waiting for his instruction, but he only nodded like the rest of them and looked to Kate.

Soon the students were going through their paces as Kate and Diego watched, giving instruction as necessary.

Kate found her eyes drawn to Diego time and again. He'd had the chance to take over the lesson, and he clearly had the skills and the connection with the kids. Still, he'd let her take charge without a peep. She wanted to thank him for trusting her abilities but kept her thoughts to herself. If she had any hope of waiting until the time was right, she needed to control her mouth and her heart.

Easier said than done.

Eventually she found herself leaning on the fence along with the children who were waiting their turn with Diego. They all watched the students and horses going slowly through the cloverleaf pattern around the three barrels, as she had just taught them. Without taking her eyes off the kids on the animals, she said, "You seem mighty popular."

She could hear Diego's smile in his words when he answered, "They're good kids. I used to help Pop give lessons whenever I could."

"When did that stop?" she asked, already knowing the answer.

She could see him fidgeting uncomfortably out of the corner of her eye. "He didn't need my help as much anymore," he explained.

He hadn't actually said it, but she knew her suspicions were correct: he'd stopped coming around after she moved in. *Because* she moved in. He seemed to know what she was thinking because he moved toward the waiting children and pulled them in for a few reminders before their turns, cutting off their conversation and creating distance between them.

Her heart went out to Diego as she watched him remind Theo how to settle into his saddle properly. Pop was right; Diego was born to do this. It was obvious he loved it.

The lesson went by in a flash, and soon they had begun the next class. Each flowed as smoothly as the one before. Kate was pleased with how well she and Diego worked together. On more than one occasion, all it took was a glance between them to communicate. Kate had never worked so well with another person. The warm glow inside her seemed to burn hotter by the minute.

After the last class was over and they were alone, Kate felt hot and tired and happy and sad all at once. She was sad because working with Diego felt so great and right, but she couldn't tell him why and it was eating her up inside.

Everything about her yearned to say the truth out loud, despite all the reason and logic that told her to wait. Because one thing was clear: she didn't want to screw up this relationship by moving too quickly. It was too important for that.

Still, every time she looked at him, she felt a burning desire to fold herself into his arms. She didn't know how she could be around him every day and pretend to *just* be friends. Not with that kiss and these heart gymnastics constantly hanging between them, along with the suspicion that he felt the same way and would do nothing about it because of Jose. They both knew Diego couldn't betray his twin brother.

For the thousandth time, she wondered how things would've been different if she'd met Diego first. The thought of Diego being on the other side of a proposal made her heart wrench.

"Are you coming to the house for lunch?" Diego asked her once they'd settled all the horses.

She felt a million things, but hunger definitely wasn't one of them. And she needed some space to breathe without worrying about getting a whiff of that masculine, woodsy smell that she'd already come to associate with Diego. "I'm going to stay out here a little longer," she told him.

He gave her a look of curiosity, but only nodded and turned away.

Kate waited until he was gone, then sighed and went to her favorite place to visit whenever she was feeling confused. Soon Darling was munching on a carrot and Kate was scratching her behind the ears. "This is so hard, Darling," Kate told the foal. The foal shook her head and snorted. "There's nothing I can do about it, so it's no use telling me what a bad idea it all is," Kate responded.

Darling still seemed skeptical. "The crazy possibility that we can make it work at some point in the future, as ridiculous as that is to hope for, is the only thing keeping me here," she explained.

Darling snorted a little. "Okay," Kate conceded. "Diego *and* you are keeping me here. And all the others. I feel at home here, but I know I might be setting myself up for a bad heartbreak in the end."

The horse nuzzled Kate's hand and Kate hugged her around the neck. "Maybe it *would* be better for everyone if I just left now, before it gets any worse," she told the animal.

"You can't leave!" Cassie said from behind her.

Kate jumped and spun around. “Cassie, what, why—” Kate began, unable to form full sentences in her confusion and surprise.

“I came by to check on Pop and thought I’d see how you were doing.” Cassie gave her friend a look of concern. “It sounds like Ma was right to be concerned if you’re talking to a horse about leaving.”

Kate considered lying, but she needed to talk to someone, even if she didn’t confess everything.

“Jose and I broke up,” she began, choosing her words with care.

“And you feel like you need to quit because you broke up with him,” Cassie mused.

Kate felt tears welling up in her eyes as she nodded. She couldn’t explain what was going on with Diego, not to someone so intimately connected to the McNeals, but Cassie didn’t push for more details. She just pulled Kate into a tight hug, and a few of the tears escaped as Kate hugged Cassie back. After a few moments, Cassie said, “You’re wrong, you know.”

Kate leaned away and looked at her friend’s face, trying to figure out what she could mean by that.

“Your job is safe here,” Cassie explained. “Nobody would ever ask you to leave this ranch because you followed your heart.”

Wanna bet? Kate thought to herself with a bit of humor. Breaking off an engagement with one son and confessing her attraction to another in the span of two days would tax even Ma and Pop’s seemingly inexhaustible love and understanding.

“I’m serious,” Cassie said, in response to Kate’s expression. "Give the McNeals some credit. They love you because of who you are, not because you were dating Jose. They'll get over the fact that you won't be giving them grandbabies," Cassie told Kate with a wink.

Kate stifled the sigh. Oh, babies. She could give them grandbabies if…

But this wasn't the time to go down that road.

Kate just smiled and thanked her friend. What else could she do? There was no way to confess what was really going on without causing all sorts of drama and commotion, but it was just so hard keeping all this to herself. She longed to confide in somebody. Say the words aloud.

Because she knew the truth now. She couldn't hide the fact of it any longer: the way she felt for Diego wasn't just a silly crush. This was straight-from-a-movie, all-capital-letters LOVE.

Chapter 8

Diego ate a sandwich alone at the kitchen table. Ma and Pop were over at Brock and Cassie's house, enjoying time with the twins. The big house surrounding Diego felt too large and empty with just him. He knew he should get to work in the office, that his email was bursting with tasks that would make or break the rodeo stock business, but every fiber of his being wanted to go back outside.

The blistering heat, the students all enthusiastically riding and learning and Kate. Everything he wanted in life was out there. He would happily take care of the school's small amount of paperwork if it meant he could have all that.

But he had obligations, and the obligation that topped the list was always to Jose. There was no way

Diego would abandon or betray his brother, regardless of what he wanted.

So Diego stood up with a big, creaking heave, feeling twice his age. He sighed and headed into the office.

After two hours of almost painfully dull work, Diego pushed his chair away from the desk and looked out the window. There was still so much to do, but he couldn't gather the motivation to actually do it.

He pulled Pop's check ledger into the center of the desk. The day before he had learned how much money was coming in through the riding school; it seemed he should understand how much was going out, too. Diego imagined a day where the horses and lessons and some simple bookkeeping were his only responsibilities, and smiled. That would be a good day.

But then Kate's face appeared and overshadowed all the rest. How could he work beside her every day, doing nothing but silently falling more and more in love with her?

The idea of being so close but so far from his desire was too much. Better to not think about it. He turned to the laptop and opened his email, hoping to distract himself with mindless productivity.

The first thing he saw was a new message with the subject line Cattle Delivery Details.

Diego opened it, puzzled, but the body of the email only made him more confused.

What the hell? he thought.

Diego pulled out his phone and started dialing. "Jose?" he said, putting his phone to his ear. "I just received an email from a Mr. Swenson about a dozen head of cattle he's expecting to be delivered next Friday."

Diego closed his eyes, and took a deep breath as his brother talked. "No, you didn't tell me. This is the first I've heard about it," he answered.

Another pause as he listened to Jose's response. "It's fine," Diego finally said with a sigh. "I'll get it taken care of."

After a few more seconds, Diego hung up his phone and rested his forehead on his hand. If Diego wasn't already sitting, he would've needed to find a chair. He had to somehow conjure up a load of animals in a hurry, all while managing a good enough deal on the purchase to make this agreement profitable. It was going to take hours to fix, and it was all for a stupid business he hated, anyway.

Diego pushed the chair away from the desk and left the tiny office. He could only think of one place he wanted to be. And one person he wanted to talk to.

Kate stabbed the pitchfork into the hay and wiped beads of sweat from her forehead. She'd spent the past few hours dealing with her feelings the way she always had: by working so hard she forgot everything but her sore arms and tired bones.

Except this was one of those rare times when it wasn't working. The barn was cleaner than it had ever been, probably. Every surface had been scrubbed and the horses had enough food and water that they'd likely be good for the next millennium or so.

No matter what she did, though, she couldn't stop

picturing Diego, couldn't get rid of the urge to go into the house and confess her feelings. Tell him she loved him and let the chips fall where they may. She'd always been an honest, forthright person, and holding herself back was driving her crazy.

Teaching students with him felt right. It was the first time she had ever found herself thinking that she'd be happy doing just this forever. Perfectly content. And that thought was wonderful and incredibly scary.

Because what if she let herself fall deeper and deeper, only to find out that Diego wouldn't or couldn't be with her?

How was she going to work with him every day without doing something foolish? It almost seemed kinder to confess and leave now than wait until it became unbearable—though she tried to ignore the voice that told her it was too late for that.

But Kate knew Diego wouldn't be able to run everything all on his own, not while running his and Jose's rodeo stock business at the same time. Could she leave the McNeals in the lurch like that?

But she had to tell him. She couldn't keep all this inside her. She would go crazy if she tried.

Kate sighed and pulled the pitchfork out of the hay, stabbing it back in as hard as she could one more time for good measure. Then she hung it on the wall and walked to the barn door. She turned and gave the horses one more look, trying to steel herself for the possibility that she might be making a very, very bad decision.

Still, she had made that decision, and she spun around, her muscles ready to move her to the house and get this over with as soon as possible. Before she could actually make good on that intention, however, her body hit a wall of clothes and skin and muscle that had appeared out of nowhere, sending her sprawling.

"Oh, God, sorry," a deep and oh-so-familiar voice rumbled.

From her spot on the ground, Kate looked up with surprise. Diego was standing over her, his hand extended to help her up. Without pausing to think, she took it, and in a second she was standing mere inches from him, her hand still in his. Electricity shot through her from that point of connection, and before her brain could catch up with her body, she was leaning into him, standing on her tiptoes and curling her free arm around his neck in an attempt to reach his mouth.

For the second time, their lips met. Just like the first time, fireworks exploded behind her eyes as she felt the pressure of him against her. Every nerve in her body melted as his hand ran down her back, then up to her neck and into her hair. She gasped with the intensity and pressed herself against him harder, feeling the body underneath the thin layer of clothing. Her hand moved from his and joined her other one on his chest.

She began unbuttoning his shirt, from the top down. She had finished the third button before she felt him begin to pull away from her and she realized what was happening.

They pushed apart at the same time, and Kate leaned against the door frame of the barn, breathing heavily. Diego was staring at her in what looked like shocked horror, his shirt half-open across his chest.

She covered her face. That was *not* how she wanted that to go. How had that happened? It was all so fast.

It was all so wonderful.

Finally, after a few seconds, she looked up at him again. He was sucking in deep breaths like he'd run a marathon. "You… That was an accident. You probably thought I was Jose and old habits die hard," he said, as if prompting her.

Kate considered agreeing with him, but she couldn't. Even if she hadn't already been convinced about where her heart was, that kiss would have done it for her. "No, Diego. It wasn't an accident."

Diego stood there staring at her. It was clear he didn't know what to say to that. Kate forced herself to keep talking. "I was going to try to wait to talk to you about this until after Jose had moved on, but—"

Her words finally seemed to bring him back to life, but not in a way Kate liked. Diego began shaking his head and buttoning his shirt. She paused and waited, already knowing what he was going to say.

"Kate, I think you're a wonderful employee," he said, earning a small grimace from her. "But we can't have that type of relationship. We can be friends, but not more than that."

Kate didn't know how to respond. She noticed he didn't say anything about not feeling *that way* about her, and that thought gave her hope.

Without another word, he turned around and began heading away from the barn. Before he got too far, though, she caught up to him. She couldn't talk about what had just happened between them, but she did have a question, and she didn't want to admit how much she hated watching him walk away. "Weren't you coming to the barn?" she asked as she caught up.

He turned and looked at her for a second, as if deciding how to word his answer. "I was just taking a little break," he said.

She couldn't leave it at that. She matched her steps to his. "What are you taking a break from? Is something wrong with your business?" she asked. His hesitation made it clear she was on the right path. "Please tell me," she said.

Diego shrugged. "It's nothing. Jose forgot to tell me about a big order and I needed to get some air before I started sorting it all out, that's all."

Kate frowned. "So Jose made this job you don't like even harder?" she asked as they entered the house.

Diego stopped, coughed, then pointed toward the office. "I have a lot of work to do," he mumbled. Then he disappeared, the door closing loudly behind him.

She almost followed him, but finally forced herself to take a seat at the table instead. She ran a finger over her lips, still puffed from the kiss. No matter what he said, she knew from the look in his eyes and the way he had kissed her that he felt *something* for her.

She had found a soul mate who wanted to be with her but wouldn't let himself.

What if she could explain things to Jose and get him to accept their relationship? If he told Diego it wouldn't hurt their brotherly bond if Kate and Diego were together, then there would be nothing stopping them.

Kate's heart inflated near to bursting at that thought.

It was a small hope, but it was hope nonetheless. She just needed to talk to Jose.

Diego entered the barn and sighed in relief. Kate wasn't there. He would get a good chunk of work done so she wouldn't be left with all of it on her own, and then she could come in and do what she liked.

For the work that took two people, well, that might need to wait a day or two until he figured something out. Maybe he could give Brock a call.

He was still reeling from the day before. That kiss was…well, it was amazing. It was what he wanted again and again for the rest of his life.

And that was why he'd decided that he needed to leave. He didn't just have a crush on her, he—

"So, where should we start?" Kate said from behind him, startling him out of his thoughts.

He turned, confused. "Didn't you get my messages?"

She smirked. "Yes, I got the text. And the email. And the note under my door."

"Then you know you can have the morning off?" he said.

Kate nodded. "There's work that needs to be done. It's my job as much as it is yours, and I don't plan on sitting around inside while you take care of all of it," she said, bringing a handful of oats over to Darling.

Diego had just assumed Kate would be embarrassed about the situation yesterday and would happily keep away from him, but apparently he'd underestimated her self-confidence or work ethic or both. It made him admire her even more.

Still, there was nothing he could do at the moment except get to work, because Kate was already moving toward one of the water buckets that needed to be dumped and scrubbed, a two-person job.

"You coming?" she asked over her shoulder.

He caught up to her, and soon they were shoulder-to-shoulder, going through the tasks for the day. "Kate—" he said, preparing for a difficult conversation.

"Did you tell Jose off for screwing up that cattle order?" she asked, cutting him off.

Diego gave her a quick sideways glance. She had stopped him on purpose, that was clear. "No. It was an innocent mistake. He didn't mean for it to happen."

They slid the large bucket to the door of the barn and dumped it. "Well, of course, he didn't *mean* to make things harder on you. That doesn't change the fact that he did, and that you shouldn't always need to clean up his messes," she told him as she grabbed two scrubbers.

Diego shrugged. "I can handle the extra work," he said. He didn't look at her when their arms touched as they cleaned the inside of the bucket. Then they hauled the bucket into place and started on the next one.

"Do you know how hard it was for Pop to give up some of the control over this place when I first got here, even though he and I both knew it was too much of a burden on him?" Kate asked Diego. "It took a good while for him to take a step back, but he was so much happier when he did." Diego wasn't fooled for a second into thinking that Kate had changed the subject. "You are Pop's son through and through, and that's a wonderful thing. But maybe you should let others take some of the burden. That's all I'm saying," Kate finished.

They stopped moving and looked at one another, and Diego felt something building in his chest. He reached up and moved a hair out of her face, hardly daring to breathe. He leaned toward her, his hand still on her cheek.

"Kate! Diego! Oh, my goodness!" Ma called as she ran into the barn.

Diego jumped back, his anticipation switching immediately to worry at the sound of Ma's voice. "Is Pop hurt?"

Ma dismissed his fears with a shake of her head. "Howie's perfectly fine. It's Amy."

"What happened to her?" he asked, anxiety clouding out any sense of reason.

"She's having a baby, Diego," Ma told him as if that should have been obvious.

"Oh, okay," he said, feeling relieved. Then what she said dawned on him. "Wait, she's having a baby *now*?"

Ma looked at him like he wasn't exactly the sharpest tool in the shed. "That's not exactly how it works, son. She's in labor, but it could take anything from a couple of hours to a day or two."

"Right," Diego responded, feeling a little stupid. To be fair, his mind was still muddled from that almost-kiss he'd just shared with Kate.

"What do you need us to do?" Kate asked, stepping into the conversation.

"Nothing yet," Ma said. "Go about your lessons and whatnot. Like I said, it should be a few hours at the very least. But I may ask you to bring some things to the hospital when it's time."

"Anything you need," Kate promised.

"Pop and I will be heading to the hospital now. To be there if Amy needs us," Ma added, as she anxiously fidgeted with her necklace.

"It'll be just fine," Diego told her, catching the nervous movement.

Ma raised her eyebrow at her son. "Of course it will be, dear. We don't live in the dark ages."

Diego smiled at the snippy response. "Fair enough," he replied.

Ma gave him a brisk nod. "I will be in touch, dears. Get back to work and have a good day," she said, giving each of them a quick kiss on the cheek before bustling back out of the barn.

Kate and Diego smiled at each other and got back to work, the moment between them broken. Diego knew that they had come very close to a dangerous moment, but it was hard to feel too guilty when a little person was making her way into the world. Right now he would enjoy Kate's company and take a break from the work and obligations that had been running his life lately.

Kate seemed content to follow his lead—they spent the rest of the time guessing how long it would take the baby to be born and what the little girl's name might be. They had both dismissed Delilah, Irene, Camilla and Sandrine.

"I'm putting my money on two in the morning and Julia," Diego said.

Kate shook her head. "You're way off. It'll be this

afternoon sometime, and something like, oh, I don't know, Darcy or something."

Diego looked up from the hay he was pitching into the stalls and squinted his eyes at her. She had said that name a little too casually. "Do you have extra information that I don't know?" he asked.

"No, not at all," she said much too innocently. "I'm just saying, if we're going to put money on it, I have a good feeling about Darcy. Want to make a friendly wager?"

Diego laughed. "No way. I know a ringer when I hear one," he said, getting back to his task.

She chuckled. "Okay, okay. Amy may have mentioned that they'd already picked the name a few weeks ago."

They finished the last of the morning's chores both smiling, and Diego felt lighter than he had in a long time. They had the animals saddled and were about to walk them out to the paddock when they caught each other's gaze for a moment. There was so much he wanted to say, so much he had to keep to himself.

Then a car door slammed and he looked up to see a car near the house. "Our first students are here," he said unnecessarily. "Do you want me to greet them or stay with the horses?"

Kate stared at him for another second before breaking contact. "You go," she said, taking the leads from him.

He gave her one last look, then followed orders.

Chapter 9

Kate was so frustrated at herself that she needed to take a few deep breaths before she started walking again. Why didn't she just say it? She'd had the chance over and over.

And Diego felt the same way. At least, she thought he did.

The consequences had stopped her, though. If he reacted the same way he'd reacted about the kiss, she didn't know what she would do. Leaving the ranch would be awful, but would she be able to just pretend she and Diego weren't crazy for each other?

Kate didn't think so. She would have to say something.

But now wasn't the time to think about all that. She pushed those thoughts to the side and focused on what she was doing. Kids were arriving and they deserved the best from her, no matter how complicated her love life had gotten.

The lessons went much like the day before—she and Diego working perfectly in sync as they went from one group to the next. The students went around the curves of the track slowly at first, then at a trot, practicing the proper signals and shifting their weight at the right times. The morning flew by, and soon it was time to bring the horses in and get some lunch.

On this day, though, she wasn't hungry at all. The thought of what she was going to say and how it might change everything made any thought of food disappear, despite having skipped breakfast that morning. She and Diego were nearly done with their time together for the day, and she knew what would happen next: he'd disappear into the office and she would be left with almost nothing to do but stew about her cowardice.

And wonder "what if." She was awfully tired of wondering that, and Diego's advice might hold true for this situation as much as for the one with her parents.

As they walked the horses to the barn, she took a deep breath. She was going to say it. She was. Any minute now.

Diego glanced at Kate as they entered the barn with the horses, curious about what she was thinking. She seemed focused internally rather than out, as if she hardly saw the world around her. Watching her, he was struck again by her beauty. The way she carried herself, the tilt of her head as she considered whatever thoughts were running around inside. Diego hated how much he hoped those thoughts were about him. She ran a finger along her lips and he nearly fell to his knees.

He looped the horses' leads around a pole, grabbed two horse brushes and started talking about whatever he could muster that had nothing to do with Kate's eyes or lips or how much he wanted to kiss her.

"Once these animals are settled, you can get back to reading *Eat, Pray, Love*. You have pretty much the afternoon off to relax. Unless Amy has her baby, in which case I'm sure Ma will expect you to be one of the first people at the hospital. She loves you like a second daughter, you know. I bet the baby won't be here for hours, and based on my nonexistent knowledge of childbirth, my guess is probably correct," he said, trying to fill the air and his wayward mind with random prattle.

"Diego, I'm in love with you," she said, standing beside the horses and looking straight at him.

Diego froze in midmovement, the brushes loose in his hands. His jaw dropped as his brain tried to process her words.

"What did you say?" he asked, certain he hadn't heard her correctly even as his heart filled to bursting.

"I know you might not want me to say it, and I was going to wait, but I just had to say it out loud," she said, shrugging. "I love you, Diego. And if there's some amount of time we need to wait before we can be together, I'll do that. But I can't pretend my feelings aren't there and they aren't going to go away, and I know you like me, too," she finished, almost as if she was asking him a question.

He looked into her emerald eyes as she stared back at him, waiting for his response. He saw the truth in those eyes. She meant exactly what she said. He had realized long ago that she was straightforward and honest, and he believed her, but he was still unable to truly accept that he was hearing what he had so desperately wanted to hear and thought he never would. "You love me?" he asked, double-checking that he hadn't invented this situation in his head.

She nodded, proving once and for all that they were both talking about the same thing. Specifically, her being in love with him.

She loved him.

They looked at each other without speaking for what felt like a very long time as his mind spun around and around with this concept. Finally, she dropped her gaze, though Diego couldn't understand why. "I'll find a new job as soon as you can find a replacement, and until then I'll just—"

As if the spell holding him in place had broken, Diego dropped the brushes, closed the space between them and pressed his lips to hers in the span of a heartbeat. She *had* to know how deeply he felt about her. And if she didn't, he would tell her with more than words.

The moment they kissed, everything suddenly felt right with the world. Anything outside of them disappeared as his hands slid into her hair. The background sounds of the barn faded to nothing when her arms linked around his neck, pulling him tighter against her. They wanted each other so badly that they hung to get everything and be at the hospital by the time we can meet the new addition."

"What everything? What are you talking about?" Diego asked, knitting his eyebrows.

"Go find Kate—she'll know. And get going! This is no time to dawdle."

With that, the line went dead and Diego stared at his phone, perplexed. He looked up at Kate, who was still in the same spot, as if she'd grown roots. "I guess we'd better go do whatever Ma told you we had to do and get to the hospital," Diego said, happy to have something to do that would help his family instead of hurt it.

Kate furrowed her brow. "What do you mean?"

"Ma seemed to think you have some jobs for us to do before we get to the hospital and that we'd better get on it," Diego replied, wondering if the stress of the situation had made his mother a little loony.

Kate seemed as confused as he was, but then understanding washed over her face. "My phone is on silent," she said, reaching for her back pocket, "so if Ma sent me— Oh, yep." Kate's eyes widened as she read her screen. "We need to get these horses taken care of and get out of here right now," she told him, and began rushing to do just that. Diego moved to help her.

Kate had more to say to Diego, but for the moment, she squashed it. They had too much to do and she was anxious to get to the hospital and meet the new baby. Kate had said she was willing to do anything for Ma, and apparently Ma had taken her very seriously because the list of tasks was long and complicated.

on as if for dear life, as if something might try to pull them apart.

They sunk into the kiss and nothing but the two of them existed for a glorious minute of heaven.

And then a voice cut through the moment like a knife.

"Well, this sucks," Jose said from the doorway.

Diego turned to see his twin glaring at them, and he felt his heart drop to his toes. Jose had never looked at him like that before. "Is this why you broke up with me, Kate? Because you've been seeing my brother behind my back?"

"Jose, it isn't like that," Diego began.

"Oh, I don't even want to hear what you have to say," Jose spat, turning to his brother. "I leave and you've immediately got your tongue down my fiancée's throat? I never thought you would do something like this."

"I'm not your fiancée," Kate said gently, putting a hand on Diego's arm to quiet him, "and our relationship wouldn't work regardless. You and I both know that."

She paused, but Jose didn't say anything. Diego wanted to do something to get that look off his twin's face, but he didn't know what he could possibly say. Before he could make any desperate promises, Kate said, "I'm sorry you had to find out like this, but I love Diego. I hope you can be happy for us."

Jose laughed and shook his head. "I can't believe this," he muttered and stormed away from the couple. Diego broke away from Kate and started after him, but he didn't get more than a few steps before Jose called back, "Don't even try to follow me, Diego!"

So Diego stood there, watching as his brother climbed into his truck, slammed the door and drove away.

Diego turned back toward Kate, and he felt his heart break as he realized that it was all over. She rushed over and hugged him, and he pressed his forehead against hers. They stood there like that, bodies together, eyes closed, foreheads touching.

Before either of them could say anything, his phone rang in his pocket, the shrill noise hardly noticeable over the sound of his thoughts. The reality they had been fighting against had broken into their fantasy world, leaving two people who had just hurt the one person Diego had promised to never hurt.

He knew it didn't matter that she loved him and he loved her. She was still Kate. And he knew that the only way to get Jose to forgive him was to stop this now.

If only that kiss could have lasted a few more seconds. Or decades. He'd give anything for a little more of that bliss. Anything except his twin brother. He couldn't give up that. Still, he wanted another second even when he knew an eternity wouldn't be enough.

Diego knew what was right, and he had to say the grim truth aloud, for both of them to hear. "Jose's my brother. My family means everything to me, but especially him. And you saw as well as I did how much we hurt him. There's no scenario where this will work, Kate."

"But what if—" she began, but he stopped her with a shake of his head. Since they were still pressed together, hers shook as well.

"No scenario, Kate. This can't happen again."

She gave a big sigh and stepped back, breaking their contact. She walked over and grabbed one of the brushes from where he'd thrown them to the floor and began tending to the horses. Diego knew she was hurting, but he could do nothing to comfort her.

"You missed a call," she said over her shoulder, keeping her back to him.

He noticed the absence of the shrill ringing that had interrupted them just a few seconds before, but he did nothing to check his phone. His arms hung limp at his sides as he watched her and wished to be in a different life. One in which he could be with this amazing woman who loved him.

If wishes were horses, he thought, patting Ricardo on the side.

Then his phone began making noise again, and this time he was in control enough to answer it.

"Why didn't you pick up earlier?!" Ma said, sounding as irritated as he'd ever heard her.

It took Diego a beat to realize where Ma was and what was going on, but as soon as he did he was on high alert. "How's Amy?" he asked.

A slew of guilt-induced worries flowed through him. What if something bad had happened to Amy or the baby, and Diego had been too occupied to answer the damn phone?

"Everything's fine. Faster than expected, even," Ma told him. "She's going into the delivery room in a few minutes. You and Kate need to leave now if you're going

After all the phone calls were made and she and Diego had stopped at a variety of restaurants, grocery stores and baby shops, Kate finally gave herself time to breathe as she settled into the passenger seat of Diego's truck. "That's everything on the list," she said, leaning back and closing her eyes for a brief moment of calm.

She heard Diego buckling his seat belt. "We should be at the hospital in about fifteen minutes," he said as he started the engine.

This is the perfect time, Kate thought, her minibreak over. She had been courageous once and it had worked until Jose walked in. Here was another opportunity.

"I want to talk to Jose about what happened, Diego," she said.

Pain flashed across Diego's face for just a second before he managed a neutral look. He didn't look in her direction. "What do you want to say to him?" he asked without expression.

Kate took a breath to calm her nerves. "I want to tell him that you and I want to be together. That we *belong* together. And that he should accept that."

There was a long silence, and Kate began to wonder if Diego would ever respond. Finally, he sighed. "I don't think that's a good idea, Kate."

She wasn't going to give up that easily. "I don't want to be left with only possibilities about you and me, Diego. Not with how great I think this could be," she said to him.

Diego abruptly turned the steering wheel and pulled into a parking lot. He stopped the truck and turned to look at Kate. She stared right back, hoping he could see the determination in her face.

"You've known Jose for a while," Diego said. "You've probably seen by now that he doesn't forgive easily."

"We can make him understand," she said, hoping he would agree, but he just shook his head.

"Kate, it's not that simple. I just hurt Jose and he may never forgive me. He's my brother," Diego said quietly.

"Your brother who flits through life and constantly leaves you to pick up the pieces," Kate blurted. "Maybe it's time you stand up and tell him you are going to live your life how you want, with the job you want and the woman you..." She paused for just a second. She was sure he loved her, somewhere deep in her soul, but he hadn't said it yet. "The woman you want," she finished, a little awkwardly.

Diego looked at Kate, knowing what she hadn't said. An image went through his mind of him saying those words to her, the future he could have with her and the riding school. But it would be without Jose.

He put his hands to his face in frustration. "You don't understand," he explained. "You don't have a twin. He's the one person I've spent my entire life with. We've been through everything together. And I owe him my life. I can't just walk away."

He could feel Kate's eyes on him. "Why do you owe him your life?" she asked at last.

"When we were young, maybe ten, we were playing up in the hayloft, I tripped and started to fall off. Jose kept his head and grabbed me. If it wasn't for him, I would have fallen twenty feet onto hard-packed ground," he said. "That's just one example. He's pulled me away from bucking horses, stood with me against bullies and told off our parents for the both of us. He has always had my back."

Kate sighed and turned to face forward. "I guess we should get to the hospital."

Diego nodded and pulled back out of the parking lot. They rode the rest of the way in silence.

Diego and Kate finally arrived at the hospital, laden down with diapers, onesies, balloons, flowers and everything else on Ma's long list of necessaries. Diego was surprised they were able to carry it all without a forklift. They tromped into the room where the rest of the family was waiting, arms spilling with gifts for the newest member of the McNeal family.

The first thing Diego noticed was Jose standing in the corner talking to Brock. He made no sign that he'd noticed his brother and ex-girlfriend walk into the room. Diego felt his guilt twist inside him, but he knew that this was not the time or place to try to fix this.

He turned his attention to Ma, who was grabbing packages out of Kate's arms, and soon the room was festooned with decorations. Diego emptied the bags he held until every available surface was covered with flowers and boxes of food, just as Ma had wanted.

As soon as everything was settled, Diego walked over to the hospital bed, where his sister and her husband sat, a teeny baby in Amy's arms. "Hey, sis," he half whispered, looking down at the little thing. "How is she?"

Amy gazed at her little baby with a broad smile. “She’s amazing,” Amy whispered back.

He watched the infant with a mixture of awe and surprise. He’d never seen a newborn before. “She’s more wrinkly than I pictured,” he told his sister, petting the baby’s head.

As Jack kneeled down and Amy handed him his daughter, he said, “She just got out of a long bath. She’ll plump up soon enough.”

Diego saw the love in the new father’s face and wondered if he’d ever experience that. He glanced at Kate and saw the wonder in her eyes as she looked down at the baby. Luckily for Diego, Brock interrupted the moment as he began poking through the packages of takeout.

“We have some chicken-curry thing,” Brock said, sniffing one container before setting it down and picking up another, “and… French toast?”

He looked quizzically at Ma.

“It’s a new twist on fried chicken and waffles, Brock. Get with the times,” Jose said, earning himself a slap on the arm from the old woman.

To everyone else, it might have sounded like Jose was being his usual funny self, but Diego could hear the edge in his twin’s voice and could only hope Jose wouldn’t blow up and ruin this moment for Amy.

Jose turned to the food packages and started opening the wide variety of options, commenting as he went. “A ham-and-cheese sandwich and taquitos. Sure, that makes sense. Ribs, coleslaw and something that looks like maple syrup. Corn on the cob. Naan. Chicken-fried rice. What's the theme?" he asked, turning to Ma.

Ma beamed. "They're Amy's favorite meals. I wasn't about to let my girl go hungry after all the work she did today. The only thing missing is my fried chicken, but I'll make that as soon as you feel up for a visit, dear," she said, turning eyes full of love on her daughter and grandchild.

Amy thanked her mother and grabbed the French toast and syrup Ma knowingly passed her way, and the rest of the family divvied up the boxes.

"So you eat French toast after having a baby," Jose mused. "What do you have after being stabbed in the back?"

Everyone stopped what they were doing to look at Jose, and Diego jumped up. "Outside, Jose," he said, ushering his twin toward the door.

Jose went begrudgingly.

Once they were out of the room with the door closed, Diego started to talk in a half whisper. "Jose, I know you're mad at me, but—"

Jose snorted, as if that didn't come close to describing how he felt. "But," Diego plowed on, "don't ruin this day for Amy, okay?"

"You didn't seem too worried about Amy when you were kissing Kate," Jose shot back.

The anger in Jose's voice cut right through Diego. "I'm sorry, Jose. I know it was wrong." Jose rolled his eyes. The next words stuck in Diego's throat. "I won't ever let it happen again. I'll get someone else to take over the riding school and get back to the city to work on our business. I hope you can forgive me," he said.

Jose ran his fingers through his hair. "I've got to go," he told Diego.

"Where?" Diego asked.

"Back to Adrianne's," Jose said.

Diego remembered why Jose had been at Adrianne's home in the first place. "Is the kid yours?"

Jose shrugged. "The results will take a few days."

Diego thought he and Jose might be able to have a normal conversation—or at least as normal a conversation as possible when it was about paternity tests—but then Jose walked away and Diego was alone in the hallway.

He took deep breaths of the sanitized hospital air. When had doing the right thing, or even just figuring out what the right thing *was*, become so difficult?

"Hey."

The word, so little but so powerful because of who the speaker was, washed over him.

Diego turned to find Kate standing just outside the closed door of Amy's room. "Hi," he said, not sure what else to say.

"Jose wasn't in a forgiving mood, I take it," she said with a little smile.

Diego leaned his back against the wall, not looking at her as she joined him. "He's never been this mad at me before," he said. He lost the ability to say the words he needed to say as she leaned beside him, their shoulders nearly touching. In spite of everything, he wanted to kiss her again *so* badly.

Wrong, wrong, wrong, he reminded himself.

"I'm going to see if Brock or Cassie can help with the riding school from now on. I need to get back to my real job," he said.

"And get away from me," she said.

Diego nodded.

"I just hate thinking 'what if,' you know? I can get over heartbreak, but I don't think I'll ever stop wondering what we could have if we gave it a shot," Kate told him, her voice cracking a little.

Diego rubbed a spot on his chest, wishing he could get rid of the ache that had lodged there. "I don't want to hurt you, but I can't risk… You and I can't—"

"I understand," she said, cutting him off.

He knew she was disappointed, but her voice was strong and steady. She was an amazingly unique woman, Kate. He heard a light *thunk* as her head dropped back against the wall.

"I'm sorry," he said.

She nodded but didn't speak. Diego wished he could do something to stop her pain, but there was nothing.

He'd done a terrible thing by betraying Jose, there was no denying that, but he was determined to be the honorable man he wanted to be. And this was a step in the right direction.

So why did it feel so wrong?

Kate tried to focus on the good things in the hospital room: the happy couple with the baby in their arms, Ma's radiant smile as she looked down at her granddaughter, the hustle and bustle of a big family celebrating a new life. Still, her heart felt like it had settled somewhere near her shoes.

Diego walked in and settled into a chair on the opposite side of the room. Kate tried not to look at him, but she couldn't help it. He looked tired and weary, as if the weight of the world was on his shoulders. Her heart went out to him, but she knew there was nothing she could do, and any attempt would just make things worse.

After a few minutes, Ma stood up. "Okay everyone," she said, getting the entire room's attention. "It's time y'all go home and let your sister and baby Darcy rest."

Kate gave Diego a sidelong glance, and she saw the corners of his lips twitch upward in a little smile as his niece's name was announced. Hers did, too.

She wanted to shout to the entire room, "I know what I want! I want Diego and love and a family!"

She wasn't letting all that go without a fight, that was for sure. And even though patience wasn't her strong suit, getting what she wanted was. She would talk to Jose and convince him, somehow.

Ma continued, "Brock, if you'll take Pop home so he can be a little more comfortable, I will stay a bit longer in case Amy and Jack need any help. Everyone else, go home and have a good day. You'll see this little one again soon enough."

With that, everyone trooped out of the room, chattering and saying their goodbyes. As Kate walked out with the rest of the family, she heard Ma call out "Diego, Kate!" and she turned around.

The older woman was standing at the doorway to Amy's room. Kate could feel Diego's presence as he stood beside her. Ma pulled them both into a tight hug that pressed them against each other. Kate could smell Diego, could feel the heat of his skin against hers. It was over all too quickly.

"Thank you both for all you did today. I can't tell you how much I appreciate it. You've done such a wonderful job," she said, planting kisses on each of their cheeks.

By the time the two of them were out of Ma's grasp and heading to the elevators, everyone else had disappeared. Diego seemed disappointed, and Kate had a guess why. She would bet good money that Diego had planned on getting her to ride with somebody else, but now he didn't have any option except to take her, which meant more time together.

Kate tried to hide her little smile as she silently thanked Ma.

Together they walked to the truck, and soon they were on the road back toward the ranch. Diego didn't seem inclined to talk, but that was fine. Kate didn't need to have a conversation with him. Just to be near him was enough.

Diego seemed to feel the opposite, because as soon as they were home, he said, "I have work to do," and disappeared.

That was okay. She had plans. First, she needed to talk to Jose. His attitude about the situation was destroying Diego, and she couldn't simply stand by and watch. Once she convinced Jose to have an open mind and that it would all be okay, then she could force Diego to reconsider his self-sacrifice on the altar of being honorable.

Kate took a deep breath, trying to ignore how insurmountable this challenge seemed.

Well, there was no time like the present. She pulled out her phone and called Jose. At the very least, if she could get him to forgive Diego, it would be a step in the right direction.

It went straight to voice mail. "This voice mailbox is full," said a robotic voice.

"Dammit," she muttered to herself.

She sent Jose a text: I know you're mad at me, but we need to talk. Call me!

Kate looked up at the ceiling and sighed. Why couldn't anything just be easy?

Chapter 10

Diego sat at the desk, not doing much at all. With all the work he had to do for that cattle order, he really needed to be making some phone calls and writing emails, but instead he stared out the window at the barn, its color fading as afternoon turned to evening. He hated how much he wanted to be out there with Kate again.

Hated it because it was a life he couldn't have, a man he couldn't be.

Finally, Diego pushed himself away from the desk, leaving the tasks he'd set for himself completely untouched. He opened the door, intent on talking to Brock about working the riding school. It was more and more clear that Diego had to get away from the ranch before he made things even worse.

He had only stepped one foot out of the room, however, when Pop's gruff voice floated down the hall toward him. "Diego? Is that you?"

Diego sighed, changed direction and went to Pop's door. "What's going on, Pop? Do you need me to grab you something?"

"I'm just fine, son, but would you mind finding Kate for me and bringing her here? I need to talk to you both. I'm supposed to rest my leg and can't get up for the life of me," Pop grumbled, clearly unhappy about being bedridden.

"Of course, you should rest," Diego agreed. "I'll go get her."

So he went off again, this time to find Kate. As much as he wanted to avoid her presence at any cost, Pop came first. He probably had something to tell them about their upcoming classes. It would be the perfect time to tell Pop his plan to get Brock to take over for a while.

It wasn't hard to find Kate; she was pacing around the living room, looking more than a little frustrated. She stopped when she saw him, and the look she gave him made Diego want to kiss her again. He also wanted to ask what she was thinking about that made her look so defiant. Regardless, he had a job to do first.

"Pop would like to see us, Kate," he told her, gesturing back toward where Pop was resting.

Kate immediately went to him, and Diego followed her back the way he'd come.

At Pop's open door, Kate gave a quick little knock, looking concerned. "You wanted to see us? Is something wrong?" she asked.

Pop waved her in. "There's only something wrong if either of you are thinking of leaving here because of that unfortunate incident in the barn," Pop said.

Diego was taken aback. How much did Pop know, and why? Diego opened his mouth, but Pop continued, "Jose talked to Brock, and well, word has spread through the family."

Diego sat down and rubbed his face, unable to believe what was happening. This was all getting worse and worse. "I'm going to talk to Brock about taking over for me here," he told Pop. "I think it's the best for everyone."

Pop glared at Diego. "I don't think that's the best for everyone at all, boy," he said.

When he called any of his sons "boy," they knew he meant business. "But—" Diego began.

"I asked *you* to take the riding school because *you* are the one who I want running things. Brock has his own work, his own land and his own family. I need you here, Diego."

Diego couldn't think of anything to say. Pop nodded, as if that settled matters, and then he turned his eyes to Kate. "And you, dear," he said in a much sweeter tone than he'd used with his son. "We want you to be here. More importantly, the school won't run without you. Tell me you're going to stay."

Kate seemed to consider for a moment, then said, "This is my home as long as you'll have me, Pop. But I'm just so sorry that—"

Pop waved his hand to stop her words. "I understand about love more than most, my dear. It's not always easy, and very often it gets a little messy. I'm not about to judge anybody as they try to find their path," he said with a little smile that made Diego wonder how exactly Pop and Ma had gotten together.

Before he could ask, all three phones in the room shrilly announced text messages.

Diego was starting to get really tired of cell phones and the interruptions they caused.

Pop picked up his first, poking it with his index finger and holding it at a distance so he could read it without his glasses. Then he looked up at the other two. "Brock saw Chester wandering around their property. He must have jumped the fence. We need to go get him," he said, moving as if he was going to try to get up and rescue the wayward horse.

"No!" Diego and Kate practically shouted in unison.

"You stay here and rest," Diego said.

"We'll get him home safe," Kate finished.

Pop didn't seem too happy with the idea of sitting around while his favorite horse was doing who-knew-what.

"I'm sure Brock is headed over right now to grab a horse and help us catch him. The three of us will be able to handle it," Kate said, patting the old man's hand.

Finally, Pop acquiesced and leaned back again, and the other two left the room at a run. They grabbed their cowboy hats and left the house. "I'll take Harry, you take Rocco?" Diego asked as they made for the barn.

Kate raised her eyebrow at him. "Rocco? I'm going to take Queen Bee, of course."

Diego had to smile. "You really love that horse, don't you?" he asked with a shake of his head.

She smiled back and Diego had to resist the urge to kiss her. It seemed like he spent half his time doing that, and the other half hiding from her. Leaving really was the best choice, he knew that, but how could he after what Pop said?

Diego felt even more lost than before, but now wasn't the time. He had Chester to think about.

He saddled Harry and hopped on, ready to find Chester and return him to his home safe and sound. "Got a rope?" Diego asked Kate as she threw herself into her own saddle.

She patted her side, where a loop of rope dangled. "I've got a halter, too. I'm not Pop, but Chester knows me well enough that I should be able to get it on him."

Diego agreed and checked to make sure his rope was secure, and then they both rode out of the barn.

"Hey, you two," Brock said, sounding out of breath from his run over. "He was out in the back pasture. Couldn't see him too well from the house and he disappeared before I could do anything, but it had to be Chester. And he seemed like he might have a problem with one of his legs."

Diego grimaced. A loose horse was one thing, but a loose *injured* horse was something else entirely. If Chester was really hurt, he might try to fight or run when they approached, and injure himself further.

He looked at Kate and her expression made it clear that she understood the dangers of the situation. "Grab a horse quick as you can and come find us," Diego told

Brock. "We're going to take a look at the paddock first, and then we'll go get Chester."

Brock nodded. Diego dismounted quickly and grabbed a first aid kit from a shelf, in case it would come in handy with Chester, and soon he was back in his saddle, the horse's hooves kicking up dust.

Kate scanned the fence line, looking for a break or anything else that might have prompted Chester's escape.

"Right there," Diego said, pointing just as she saw the same issue. A fence post had broken, leaving a gap large enough for a horse to maneuver through.

Kate scanned the rest of the horses, her hat shading her eyes from the hot sun, and checked to see who else might be loose. "Chester's the only one missing," she said, relieved that more hadn't made their way out.

Now they needed to keep it that way. "I'll get to the break and assess the damage. You go to the barn and grab what we need to do a quick repair. And let Brock know," Kate told Diego.

He turned around without a word and sped toward the barn as Kate made her way to the gap in the fence line. Once there, she looped Henry's reins around a secure part of the fence to ensure he wouldn't wander off, too, and then looked at the pieces of wood strewn across the ground.

It didn't seem like anything big. The post had snapped near the bottom, likely from normal wear and then a push from a big wind or a kick from an animal.

But they'd need to check the rest of the fencing for termites in the next few days.

For now, they could prop up the old post, tie it to the broken bit and use a few nails to keep everything together until after they got Chester back.

Kate braced herself to lift the big post back into place. It would be tricky to get it in the right spot, but she thought she could do it and there wasn't any time to spare. With a heave, the post was standing up.

Now, to secure it. She pulled the rope from her belt and kneeled down to tie the broken portion to the part that was still stuck in the ground. When she bent over, though, the post wobbled, and even though she stood quickly to grab it, it was too late: the heavy piece of wood toppled over and slammed to the ground, scraping against her arm on the way down.

She inhaled with a hiss as pain washed through her. A look at her left arm made it obvious what had happened: a nail or something on the post had sliced her skin when it hit her, leaving a long, bleeding gash.

Diego rode up while she was inspecting her arm. "What happened?" he asked as he dismounted and walked quickly over to her.

"I was trying to fix the fence," Kate began, but her voice faltered when Diego's warm hands touched her arm with tender care.

Diego shook his head, her eyes still on the wound and the blood dripping down her elbow. "Why didn't you wait for me?" he asked.

Kate didn't have a good answer for that. "I guess I'm

just used to getting things done on my own, and we're in a rush," she finally answered.

Diego didn't seem too pleased about that, but he didn't say so. He just opened the first-aid kit and pulled out some gauze. "I guess it's a good thing I grabbed this, even if it doesn't help Chester any. Though you'll want Cassie to disinfect it when we get back. Maybe even give you a few stitches. Unless you think you need to go see her now?" he asked, looking into her eyes with concern.

Kate shook her head. "I'm fine, really. And I should be around when we find Chester. Let's fix this thing so we can go get him," she said.

After Diego wrapped the wound, he and Kate quickly fixed the fence enough to keep any other horses from wandering off. Kate grimaced when she moved her arm but didn't say anything. Diego gave her a quick glance. "Injuries are already common enough on a ranch. You shouldn't put yourself into more danger by trying to get by without help," he said.

"Well, if it makes you feel better, I'm afraid I won't be able to do much work tomorrow," she told him with a scowl.

Diego smiled at her. "That'll teach you a lesson. If you get injured, you can't work."

She laughed at how silly it sounded, but it was true. Sitting around while Diego took care of the horses without her was going to drive her crazy, and they both knew it.

Brock joined them just as they finished the task. "Cassie called. She said that Chester came into view on the far side of the pasture for just a minute, then disappeared into the trees. And he's definitely limping."

Kate and Diego both hoisted themselves into their saddles, Kate managing it one-handed, and then all three of them were beating a trail to Brock's back pasture. They didn't want to lose any more time—the longer Chester was out, the more trouble he could get into and the harder it would be to catch him and get him home.

Kate, Diego and Brock scoured the back pasture for several minutes, searching carefully in the place Cassie had seen him. Finally they found Chester munching on some grass, calm as could be.

Kate hopped down, tossed her reins to Diego and approached the horse slowly. She murmured calming words as she pulled a handful of oats from her pocket, careful not to startle him. Chester looked at her and limped over, clearly avoiding pressure on one of his front hooves.

Once he was close enough, Kate slipped the halter around his neck, then gave him a pat. She was about to attempt to check the problem leg, but then stopped. This wasn't something to do alone when there were more people around. Especially since she was injured.

Kate looked over at Diego and Brock, who had dismounted. Diego gave her a smile, handed the reins to Brock and walked over to where she and Chester stood. "Need some help?" he asked.

Kate smiled. "That would be nice, thank you," she said with an embarrassed smile.

Diego lifted Chester's leg. "Just a big rock," he said,

sounding relieved. "He might be a little sore, but he's fine."

After the rock was removed from Chester's horseshoe, Kate tied Chester's halter to her saddle, and soon the three people and four horses started trooping back home. "We're going to drop by your house first," Diego told Brock. "We need Cassie to take a look at Kate's arm."

Kate wanted to roll her eyes, but she couldn't. It was wonderful having someone worried about her, someone who cared.

When they reached the house, Cassie came out to greet them. "Looks like he's okay," she said with a smile.

"Yeah, but Kate needs you to take a look at her arm. She sliced it while fixing the fence," Brock told his wife.

Cassie waved Kate off her horse. "Come on in. I have some disinfectant. Hopefully it isn't too deep," she said, the doctor in her taking over.

Kate tossed her reins over to Diego a second time. He still seemed a little concerned. "I'm fine. You can take QB back to the barn and I'll meet you there. Be back in a jiffy," she told him.

Cassie pulled Kate into her examination room and started unwrapping the bandage, making little tsking noises as she went. "Well, I've seen worse," she proclaimed once she'd gotten a good look at the wound, "but that doesn't mean you shouldn't be more careful. I'll clean it and glue it together and it should heal up just fine."

Kate didn't want to annoy this doctor version of Cassie, so she didn't make any sarcastic comments about being glued back together and waited patiently for the doctor to do her thing.

Cassie swiped on some disinfectant that made the cut burn, but Kate held her tongue. It was a bad idea to curse at her friend. Cassie turned away and grabbed a little tube of something or other. As she worked on the wound, she said, "So, you didn't tell me the whole story."

"What do you mean?" Kate asked, staring at her arm. "Something on the post scraped me."

"Not about that. About you and Diego. You didn't tell me about *that* when I visited you in the barn," Cassie said.

Kate blushed, but luckily Cassie kept her eyes trained on what she was doing. "I can't believe the entire family knows about that," Kate said.

She wanted to pack her bags and go every time she thought about Jose describing what he'd seen, as if it was some tawdry thing and she was just a girl who made out with any guy in a mile radius. She felt so much for Diego; how would she make them all understand?

Cassie snorted in a very undoctor-like fashion. "Jose isn't one to keep his mouth shut, in case you haven't noticed. You and Diego have it bad for each other, don't you?"

Kate sighed. "Life would be so much easier if we didn't," she said.

Cassie gave her a sympathetic smile. "Love doesn't always work that way," she said.

"Is Ma going to hate me forever because of what I've done to her sons?" Kate asked, finally confessing the fear she'd had since Pop told her that they all knew about the incident in the barn.

Cassie's smile turned amused. "I haven't talked to her, but I have a feeling she saw this coming before you did," she said.

Kate wanted to ask what she meant, but before she could, Cassie asked, "So, what are you going to do?"

Kate shrugged, then regretted the decision as a pain shot through her arm from the movement. "If I can talk to Jose about what happened, get him to understand that we weren't trying to hurt him and that Diego and I have real feelings for each other, then maybe Diego will stop feeling like he's betraying his brother anytime he's near me and maybe things could work out between us."

Cassie didn't seem too optimistic. "That's a big *if*, Kate. We all know Jose—"

"Yeah, I know." Kate sighed. "But I can't just give up."

Cassie put a hand on Kate's uninjured arm. "I'm rooting for you, however all this turns out," she said. Then she became the doctor once more. "You're all patched up. Try not to move your arm much for an hour or two, and give it a break for a few days. You should be good as new in no time."

Kate hopped off the examination table. "Thanks, Doc. What do I owe you?"

"You owe me a pastry from the bakery and some time to chat in the next week or two," Cassie said with a smile.

Kate hugged her friend and left, only to find Diego and Brock still waiting for her with the horses. "I thought you'd be at the ranch by now," Kate said.

Diego seemed a little embarrassed, and Kate could

see he had been worried about her and hadn't wanted to leave until he was sure she was fine. It was endearing, and if she wasn't already so in love with him, she might've fallen for him right then and there. "Thanks. Now I don't have to walk back," she said, slipping into her saddle.

Diego tipped his hat at her as he got back in his own saddle, and the two of them set off with Brock toward their barn, pulling Chester along behind them.

As they rode to the house, Brock talked about possible options for fixing the fence. Diego and Kate didn't say much, but Brock either didn't notice or didn't mind. Once they reached the McNeal ranch, Diego turned to Kate. "We'll take care of the horses and then work on the fence. Will you go let Pop know what happened?" he asked.

Kate looked down at her arm. "I guess that's all I'm good for right now, since I'm supposed to let my arm rest. Doctor's orders."

Diego was glad to hear that was the case, because between his promise to Jose and Pop's wish that he stick around, Diego's only option seemed to be as little time around her as he could possibly manage. When he was near Kate, he let himself think about what could've been, and that was dangerous.

Staying away from her was the honorable choice, as much as it hurt. What made it even more difficult was that he could see that Kate hadn't given up on him yet. So not only was he fighting against his own heart, but he also had to stay strong in the face of her stubborn determination—no easy task. So all in all, Diego was glad that he could spend the day outside and that she was on orders to rest.

Diego and Brock brushed down and settled all four horses into their stalls. Then they gathered the supplies they would need for the fence and drove it all over in the bed of Diego's truck.

"So," Brock said as he relaxed in the passenger seat, "sounds like you're going to stick around for a while?"

Diego half nodded. He honestly wasn't sure if he should leave or not, regardless of what Pop said—the longer he stayed, the harder it would be for everyone. He wasn't sure Jose would ever forgive him as it was, let alone if he thought Kate and Diego were still up to funny business.

Which they weren't and would never be, Diego thought sadly.

"How long have you been in love with Kate?" Brock asked as they stepped out of the truck and surveyed the fence.

Diego sighed. There was no use pretending, especially since Brock was well aware of what Jose had seen. "Since the day I met her."

Brock nodded. "Do you think Jose will forgive you?"

Diego shrugged. "I think if I can get him to see that I'm sorry and won't ever do anything like that again, he'll come around eventually. But I think it's going to take a long time," he said.

And a lot of heartache, he thought to himself, stopping the truck beside the broken fence.

Brock opened his door and climbed out. "I sure hope he'll take the high road on this one. For your sake."

Diego gave a sad laugh. "That's not his strong suit," he said.

Brock rolled his eyes in agreement. "Yeah, he's not the most forgiving person. Still, you can't help who you fall in love with. I know that better than anyone," he said, looking back toward his ranch, where Cassie and the twins were probably waiting for him to get home.

Diego felt a pang slice through his heart at the thought. He started talking, unable to stop the flood of thoughts that he could finally say to somebody. "I know it's terrible. We've been so close all our lives and I can't believe that I'm in love with Kate. It's wrong and I know it."

Brock heaved a heavy piece of lumber from the truck bed. "I don't know what to tell you. I'm not going to lie and say that Jose will ever be fine with it. We both know that he probably won't forgive you if you carry on with her."

Diego nodded. He knew how his brother could be. He was a goofball, sure, but he also had a jealous streak and was hotheaded if he felt himself wronged. And this was certainly one of those situations.

"Still," Brock continued. "Love's love. You'll need to do what you think is best. Now, help me get this thing fixed," Brock finished as he hoisted up the new post.

Diego and Brock repaired the fence in silence while Diego thought about what his older brother had said.

Despite Brock's advice, Diego didn't know what the best course of action could be. He knew what the honorable thing to do was, but was that the same as the best? He really couldn't say. If he had a relationship with Kate despite Jose's objections, he would lose his twin and lifelong best friend. But he and Kate had something amazing, he knew that, and living a life without her seemed hardly worth living at all.

Once they were done, Brock walked back to the truck, but Diego stayed near the fence. "I think I'll walk along the fence line and check for any weak points," he told Brock, tossing him the keys. "You can take the truck back. I might be a couple of hours."

Brock caught the keys and shook his head. "I hope you figure this all out, Diego."

Then Diego was alone, and happy to have the time to think.

Kate looked at her phone in frustration. She had texted Jose again. And again and again. Since he wouldn't answer her calls, she had resorted to sending him messages explaining that she and Diego made sense together, loved each other and wanted to be together. She said she hoped he could find it in his heart to accept them as a couple. She said that Diego was willing to put Jose's happiness above his own and lose this great thing they could have.

She said all that and more, hoping some of her words would get through the wall of anger Jose had erected.

So far, she had heard nothing back from him. Not a single message. For all she knew, he'd thrown his phone in a lake and her passionate entreaties were only being read by crabs and fish.

Kate wanted to throw her phone at the wall. She just wanted to get this whole thing sorted out so she could follow her heart. She knew where it led.

For the first time in her life, she knew exactly who she wanted, and she wasn't about to let him go without a fight.

Kate's phone beeped in her hand, and she looked down at it in surprise. Was it Jose, responding to her messages? Was it Diego saying something, anything?

It was Ma.

Hello, dear. Would you mind bringing me a few things at the hospital? I'm going to stay the night.

Kate smiled at the list of necessities, which included a toothbrush, nightgown and Amy's favorite dessert. That was a doting mother right there.

The front door opened, and Kate looked up to see Brock walking into the house. "I'm just dropping off Diego's keys," he told her, placing them on a hook near the door.

"Where's Diego?" she asked.

Brock gave her a look that made it all too clear he knew why she asked. "He's walking the fence line looking for any other weak spots. It could be a couple of hours," he said.

After Brock left, Kate messaged Diego about the trip to the hospital and then began to gather Ma's things. By the time he wrote back, she was sitting on the couch, bouncing her foot up and down impatiently.

I'll still be a long while. Take my truck. Unless you aren't feeling well and need me to go for you?

Kate could read between the lines clearly enough. He didn't want to be around her. She understood why, but it didn't make it hurt less.

Kate grabbed the keys and stormed out of the house. These McNeal men were driving her crazy. At least at the hospital she could be around Ma and Amy, who would hopefully talk about nothing but the new baby.

Kate couldn't wait.

When she knocked on the door to Amy's room to announce her arrival, Ma came rushing over to her. "Dear! Pop told me what happened to your arm. You should have just stayed home and rested," she said in a loud whisper.

"I'm fine," Kate said, trying to hide her grimace as she set down the bag of things she'd brought, pulling at the wound in the process. "It's nothing, really," she added at the expression on Ma's face. "I wanted to come see the baby."

Ma bustled Kate into the room and over to Amy's bed, where Amy was dozing. Darcy was sleeping in a crib near the bed. Kate looked down at the baby and felt her heart melt as she looked at the tiny thing.

"Isn't she wonderful?" Ma whispered as she placed a hand on the baby.

Kate had to agree. For some reason she didn't want to examine too closely, Kate felt her eyes sting with tears.

Ma gave her a sympathetic grin. "You'll have one soon enough, I'm sure," she said before turning to the packages Kate had brought.

Kate felt a pang. It sounded like Ma didn't know the chaos Kate had created in her family. In all likelihood the woman would be devastated if she knew Kate was coming between her two boys like this, and Kate didn't have the heart to tell the older woman. She'd find out sooner or later, but for now maybe everything could just be okay.

"I'm going to go freshen up, dear," Ma told Kate, and with a quick pat on the good arm, she was gone and the room was silent.

Kate sat on a stool near the baby's crib and looked down at the tiny one. "I hope I get to be around to see you grow up, Darcy," Kate said quietly. "Things are a bit complicated right now, though. If I miss it, I'm still rooting for you."

"I don't think the word *complicated* does justice to what's going on in your life, Kate," Amy said, looking much more awake than she had just a few moments ago.

Kate wanted to stomp her foot in frustration. She had been looking forward to a bit of time not focused on her messy life, and yet she had been the one to bring it up immediately. "I thought you were sleeping," Kate said.

"I wasn't," Amy answered cheerily. "Did Jose really catch you and Diego going at it in the barn?"

Kate sighed. "We were kissing, yes," she admitted.

Amy seemed disappointed. "Oh, I thought…never mind. That's still interesting."

Kate could feel her cheeks burning. This was getting more out of control by the second.

"So, dated one twin and now in love with the other, right?" Amy asked.

Kate nodded, and Amy let out a little whistle. "Jose's pissed," she said.

"I know," Kate said. "I've tried to talk to him and explain things, but he's not answering his phone."

Amy seemed to understand it was time to stop making light of the situation. "Give it time, Kate. This has to be really hard for him."

Kate wanted to cry. "I didn't want to hurt anyone," she said, falling into a chair.

"We all know that," Amy said sympathetically. "And hopefully, deep down, Jose knows that, too."

Kate's emotions broke over her like a tidal wave and she began to sob. For herself and Diego and all the hurt she had brought onto this family. Hopelessness broke over her, stronger than it had since she'd woken up kissing Diego.

"I was hoping we would talk about the baby and not my train wreck of a love life," she finally said with a tearful laugh.

"We can talk about other things," Amy assured her as Kate wiped her eyes.

The baby started to whimper just as Ma reentered the room. "Jack should be back any minute with food for everyone," she said.

Amy picked up the baby from the little crib beside the hospital bed and started to nurse her. The room quieted. "So, I hear things have been eventful over at the ranch, Kate. Are you okay?" Ma asked.

Does she know everything? Kate wondered. It didn't take her long to find out.

Ma pulled Kate into a big hug. "Don't worry, dear. I'm sure Jose will come around and see how good you are for Diego."

Kate heard Amy make a noise in her throat. "Ma, don't raise Kate's hopes like that. You know Jose as well as anyone," she said.

Ma gave her daughter a stubborn look. "I've worked plenty hard to get these kids matched up properly, and if Jose thinks throwing a fit is going to—"

"Wait, wait, wait," Kate broke in, astonished. "What do you mean 'matched up'?"

Ma looked a little embarrassed, but defiant. "It was obvious you and Diego should be together from the start," Ma explained.

"What did you do, Ma?" Amy said, sounding exasperated.

"Nothing!" Ma exclaimed. "I just gave you both a few nudges here and there."

Kate thought over all the times she and Diego had wound up spending time together and wondered how many of them had been orchestrated by Ma. There was the ridiculous list of stuff needed for the hospital room, the way she'd called them back as everyone headed to the elevators, and then another situation popped into her head. "Ma, did you tell Diego he should sleep in Amy's room that night?" she asked.

The answer was written all over Ma's face. "I hoped maybe you'd both see what I had known all along. I thought that maybe if you two saw each other in your skivvies—"

"Ma!" Amy exclaimed.

"Oh, God," Kate said, wishing she had stayed home to rest.

"Listen, Kate," Ma said softly. "I'm sorry if I pushed

too far. I just *know* you and Diego are right for each other. I know it down to my bones."

Kate gave Ma another hug. She was right about her and Diego, but would optimism and hope be enough, or were there just too many complications?

Kate took a deep breath.

"I'd rather not talk about any of this right now, if you don't mind," she told the women.

They nodded, and everyone turned their attention to Darcy, who was looking up at them with wide newborn eyes. The rest of Kate's visit was spent cooing over the baby as Amy regaled her with the gritty details of childbirth.

Kate tried to focus, but her thoughts kept going back to the triangle orchestrated by this sweet old woman.

If only she could be confident it would all turn out the way she hoped. At least, she decided, she would try.

Chapter 11

Diego had successfully avoided Kate the entire afternoon and evening, and he went to bed exhausted from his day's work. Even so, he found it hard to sleep. And when he slept, he dreamed of Kate.

He couldn't be with her. He knew that. There were some things a man just didn't do, and this was one of them. He refused to put his own happiness over that of his family, and Jose was more his family than anyone on earth.

If only doing the right thing didn't feel so damn awful.

The next morning, he rose from bed, weary and worn. He hoped and prayed Kate would stay in the house and rest, but if she was out there trying to work, she needed help and he couldn't leave her to struggle through it alone. He was better than that.

So he pulled on his jeans and boots, his shirt and hat, and left the house as quietly as he could. He would do the work, try not to get in her way and survive somehow. Once the horses were cared for and the day's classes were over, he would consider what he needed to do next. Whatever it was, it would need to involve as little contact with Kate as possible.

She was already in the barn, waiting for him, just like he knew she would be. "You should go back to the house and rest your arm," he said, even though he knew how she was going to answer.

Kate raised an eyebrow. "I work here, and I'm not going to stop doing my job because of a little scratch," she told him.

He shrugged and grabbed a shovel. "Wait," she said, grabbing his arm. "We need to talk."

That was the last thing Diego wanted to do. "About what?" he asked.

"About us, Diego. You can't pretend you don't have feelings for me," she said.

"It doesn't matter if I do or not," he said, feeling his heart tear into pieces. "Jose—"

"Yes, he's your twin and he's mad and there's nothing we can do about that right now. He'll get over it," she said. Her eyes were on fire as she said it, all confidence and strength. God, he wanted to kiss her.

"I don't want to give this up," she persisted, squeezing his arm.

"This isn't anything, Kate," he said, praying she would accept the lie, as much as it hurt to say.

"This is everything!" she almost shouted. She waved

her arms around her. "This ranch! My job! My students! And you," she said, walking up to him. "More than anything else, I don't want to give up you, because *you* are everything."

Any argument he could have made died on his lips when Kate pressed hers against them.

He wanted her so badly, wanted to believe that it was possible, that it was right.

And the part of his mind that told him he shouldn't was so easy to ignore when her body was against his.

Diego couldn't fight against the flood of fire in his veins. Finally, inevitably, he let himself go. His hands ran across Kate's back, memorizing every curve. They went further and found a woman who was more than willing, almost demanding his touch.

They gave and took, their pent-up passion desperate for release.

Afterward, they were lying on an old blanket on the floor of the barn, and Diego wrapped his arms tight around Kate, never wanting to let go.

And he didn't think he would ever let go. This was the kind of love you only got once in a lifetime. It was something that should be shouted from the rooftops. The very least he could do right now was finally admit it.

"I love you," he said aloud, feeling the weight of the words as he said them.

"I love you, too," she told him, her clear green eyes focused entirely on him.

They stared into each other's eyes for a long moment,

and he finished what he had to say before he lost the will. "But this was wrong. I have to be a better man than this."

Kate looked at him, her mouth open slightly, and all he wanted to do was kiss away the pain he saw on her face. "I'm sorry, Kate, but I can't be around you anymore. It's too hard. I hope you understand."

Kate stood up to dress, and he wanted nothing more than to pull her back down beside him. "I hope you can forgive me," he said.

Kate turned on him, her eyes shining with tears. "You know what it is? You're so damn worried about the right and honorable thing that you're willing to give up everything good in your life. Jose will forgive you. He's your *brother*. But you can't forgive yourself."

He let her anger crash over him, taking it as fair punishment for his mistakes. There was a long silence as she finished dressing.

"The students will be arriving soon," she said quietly. "I expect you to help me with classes today. After that, leave or do whatever you think is the 'right' thing to do."

Kate stormed out of the barn and stomped her way toward the house. He watched as she left, his heart twisting itself to pieces.

Diego took a deep breath, dressed and started to saddle the horses.

Diego finished the task in a daze. He felt almost overwhelmed by guilt—guilt for hurting Kate and guilt for betraying Jose, the two of them competing for dominance inside him.

By the time Kate reentered the barn with damp hair

and fresh clothes, the horses were saddled and ready to go, though Diego hardly remembered doing it.

His mind was entirely focused on Kate and what had happened between them.

"The ten-to-twelve group will be here any minute," she said, her manner all business.

Diego nodded, even though all he wanted to do was grab her in his arms and tumble down to the ground again.

Without speaking, the two of them brought the horses out to where the lessons would be held that day, set up the barrel-racing course and then went to meet the arriving children. Diego didn't know how he ever managed to get through it all with his heart ground to dust beneath his feet.

Kate had never felt so angry. She didn't know if she wanted to slap Diego or kiss him again. Diego was a good guy and he was trying to do the right thing, she got that, but he was giving up too much in the name of it. And it wasn't fair.

But the students deserved her best, so Kate took a few deep breaths and gathered them near the paddock, starting the class as she always did. Her eyes wanted to drift over to where Diego stood, but she didn't let them.

Somehow she managed to get through the instructions, and the first round of students began moving through the paces—a warm-up, then slow trips through the obstacle course. Finally, each one went through individually at a trot, practicing the movements necessary to make it through the course in good form. Kate continued to call out instructions and put all her attention on the children.

Everything was going as well as could be expected until Hannah, one of the youngest in the group, was supposed to make her run through the course. Kate could see that she was freezing up and held the reins for an extra second. "Hannah, you okay?" Kate asked.

Hannah looked at her with scared eyes. "I can't do it," she said. "I'm not good enough yet."

"You are exactly as good as you need to be in order to try," Kate told her. "That's all we're asking for here, okay?"

Jonas, Hannah's older brother, shouted from the fence, where he waited for his turn. "Don't fall off, scaredy-cat!"

Hannah stuck her tongue out at her brother and faced forward. Kate let go of the reins and stepped back as the horse started to move. Everything looked good as Hannah began the first curve at a quick trot, but it quickly became apparent that something was wrong.

Hannah wobbled as she took the curve. The saddle tipped to the side, spilling the girl from her seat, tumbling her into the side of the barrel on the way down.

Kate let out a small scream before she could stop it, and she ran over to Hannah as fast as she could. Diego appeared beside her, and they both kneeled to examine the girl. Hannah was crying and clutching at her arm where she'd hit the barrel.

"She's hurt," Kate said, her heart in her throat.

"Call Cassie. Get the truck," Diego said as he carefully examined the arm.

Kate tugged her phone out of her pocket and started to make the call. "Everyone stay right where you are, even you, Jonas!" Kate called to the stunned children as she bolted toward the house, phone to her ear.

It only took a few seconds to get Cassie rushing over, and the two of them were in the truck and driving toward the paddock in no time. As they drove up, Kate felt relief sweep through her at what she saw. Hannah was curled in Diego's arms, crying but not hysterical.

She was holding her arm funny—she was definitely injured—but she didn't seem fatally hurt. Cassie jumped out almost before Kate stopped the truck, and as soon as Cassie reached the little girl she examined Hannah carefully. "You dislocated your shoulder," Cassie said. "We'll need a full examination and an X-ray to see if there are any other problems. It looks like we're headed back to the hospital," she declared, turning to Kate and Diego.

"I feel like I've been at the hospital enough to last me a lifetime," Kate joked, happy to see that Cassie didn't seem too scared.

"I'll take her. Kate, you stay with the kids. And call Hannah's parents," Diego said.

Kate looked at him, but he didn't make eye contact. He still seemed shaken up about the whole situation. She wanted to reassure him that it would be okay, but there wasn't time. Diego was already climbing into the truck with Cassie hustling behind him.

"Wait, wait!" Jonas called out, crying as he raced for the truck. Diego stood aside and let Hannah's brother jump in, and then the four of them were off.

Kate watched them go, and then she turned to the tasks ahead of her. "Everyone, we're going inside. We'll have a snack while we wait for your parents," she said as she rushed the kids away from the horses.

She would get them inside, and then she'd need to make a very unpleasant phone call to Hannah's parents.

But everything was going to be all right. It had to be, didn't it?

Chapter 12

Cassie walked into the waiting room where Diego sat, his head in his hands. When he heard her arrive, he looked up. "You shouldn't look so glum. Hannah will be just fine. It's only a dislocated shoulder," Cassie said as she sat beside him.

Diego was glad Hannah was okay, but it didn't change the guilt he felt. After all, he'd been the one who had put on the saddles. And Hannah fell because her saddle wasn't tightened properly.

Diego felt as if all the blood had drained out of him, leaving just an empty shell. Hannah had her arm in a sling because of him, and it could've been so much worse. He couldn't rid himself of the image of her hitting that barrel as she fell, or the panic that had gripped him as he rushed to her side. And it had been all his fault. If he'd been paying attention, if he hadn't been so distracted, he would've put the saddle on tightly enough and this wouldn't have happened.

Or if he had left the ranch like he'd promised Jose he would, Kate would've put the saddles on properly. But no, he'd betrayed his brother yet again with Kate that morning, and this was what happened. It was a sign, clear as day.

And he knew he'd be a fool to ignore it.

"Hey, are you all right?" Cassie asked, placing a hand on Diego's arm. Diego could only shake his head. "Why don't you head home and get some rest? I'm going to go up to Amy's floor and visit with them for a bit. They're going to take Darcy home in a few hours. I can easily get a ride."

Diego nodded and stood. "Thanks, Cassie," he said before leaving, but if she replied, he didn't hear her.

He knew the right thing to do. Now, before anything else happened. It was time to settle the matter once and for all.

Diego grabbed his cell phone and tapped on a contact quickly before he could change his mind. He held the phone to his ear, his grip on it so tight he vaguely wondered if it might break.

Kate paced around the kitchen, avoiding Pop's crutches and propped-up leg. She was unable to sit still despite Ma's insistence that she relax and have some tea. The students had all been picked up and the rest of the day's classes canceled. Now Kate had nothing to do, when all she wanted was to work.

Even though Cassie had already called and told her Hannah would be fine after a few weeks with her arm in a sling, Kate knew she wouldn't be able to settle down until she'd spoken to Diego and heard it from him. As mad as she'd been with him, she still couldn't help but want to lean on him.

And he should have been back more than an hour ago, based on when Cassie said he'd left. Kate had nearly called him a dozen times but stopped herself. He was probably driving around, thinking about all that had happened that day. She would wait until he was there in person, and then they would talk about their plan.

A phone rang, making Kate jump, but it wasn't hers. She looked over to Pop, who was fishing his phone out of his pocket with a confused look on his face. "Hello?" he asked as he put the phone to his ear.

Kate watched as his expression clouded over. "Are you sure?" he asked. After a moment, he sighed. "If you think that's best, son," he said, though he didn't sound happy about it.

Which son was he talking to? If it was Diego, why didn't he just come home, or call her? What was going on?

Kate waited impatiently for the old man to hang up the phone. Once he did, however, she couldn't make herself ask what had been said. She just waited for the bomb to drop.

Pop looked at her with a shake of his head. "Diego isn't coming back. He insisted that somebody else would need to help with the ranch. Said he was going to go home and work on his real job."

Kate sat down. So that was it. Diego really wasn't going to come around. It was over.

She wanted to throw something, but before she could storm out to the barn and do just that, Ma slapped her hand on the table. "No!" she said, so forcefully that Kate and Pop both looked at her in surprise. "I've worked too hard to get you two together. I can't come this close and let my baby choose to be miserable," she told the two of them, crossing her arms defiantly.

"I can't *force* him to love me," Kate said, feeling hopeless.

"Oh, he already loves you," Ma answered, wagging her finger at the young woman. "He just needs to realize that he *should* love you. That it's good and right and his ma is never wrong about her children and love."

Kate shook her head. "He's made his decision, and I can't blame him for it. Jose's too important to him."

Ma leaned close to Kate. "Well, I'm not giving up yet. Are you?"

Kate looked into the old woman's earnest eyes and thought about the insurmountable odds. She sighed and dropped her gaze to the table.

Her mind was running a million miles a minute, but it kept going back to the same thought again and again. Diego had just disappeared from her life, just like that. And now she was alone.

Diego sat in the little hole of an office he and Jose rented for the business. He'd tried to go to his apartment in the city, but it was too big, quiet and lonely. He felt lost there. It wasn't his home anymore, if it ever had been. His home was back at McNeal Ranch with Kate.

So he'd left and gone to the office, buying a bottle of whiskey on the way. Now he poured a glass of the brown liquid and looked at it. He'd just deal with his problems the cowboy way. He picked up the glass and brought it to his lips when he heard the door open.

Diego looked over and saw Jose making his way through the crammed space. Diego watched his brother warily, waiting for an onslaught of accusations and anger. "Hey, brother," Jose said casually as he folded his large frame into one of the two customer chairs sitting before Diego's desk, a puff of dust erupting from the never-used cushion. "Burning the midnight oil?" he asked, despite the sun shining through the tiny window.

Diego gave his twin a long look. This wasn't what he'd expected at all. Not only did Jose act like he wasn't angry, but there was also something else different about him. He was acting strange, though Diego couldn't put his finger on exactly what it was.

"What are you doing here?" Diego asked.

Jose started cleaning his fingernails, acting nonchalant. "Nothing, just thought I'd come check up on my twin. You know how it is."

"Why aren't you yelling?" Diego asked.

Jose shrugged. "Don't want to disturb the neighbors," he answered.

Diego didn't have the energy to play games. "What's going on, Jose?"

Jose looked his brother straight in the eye. "Ma called and gave me an earful. Said I was ruining your life by being a stubborn ass and that I needed to get over myself," he said.

Diego waited a beat. "And?"

Jose gave his brother a smirk. "And she's right."

Then Jose reached over, took the drink from Diego's hand, swigged the liquid and handed back the empty glass.

Diego sighed and looked at the bottle. He wished he'd started drinking a long while before, because he felt way too sober to have this conversation with his brother. Even though Jose was holding it together, Diego was sure his twin was still mad at him, as he had every right to be. And he would be even more furious if he found out what had happened in the barn that morning.

"I've betrayed you, Jose. I hope I can show you that I'm sorry and we can be close again. And you don't have to worry, I'll stay away from Kate and—"

"Stop it!" Jose shouted, drowning out anything else Diego might have planned on saying.

Diego leaned back and waited for the onslaught of Jose's anger. He knew Jose had no reason to trust him at his word and knew he deserved everything Jose was about to say. He'd betrayed Jose in a way he had vowed would never happen.

Jose didn't shout again, though. He leaned forward in his seat, so he was almost touching the desk, and looked at Diego seriously, but without anger. "I want you to listen to me very carefully, Diego. I don't need you to take care of me. I am an adult, and I'm going to finally start acting like one. If you give up Kate for me, you will be the stupidest man I've ever met."

Diego's mouth opened, but he didn't know what to say. Jose didn't need him?

"I love you, Diego," Jose continued, "but it's time for you to treat me like a grown-up and look to your own happiness. I've found mine, and the only way I'm going to keep it is if I start acting like a real adult."

"What?" Diego asked, more confused than ever.

"Adrianne," Jose said, as if that explained everything. "And Maisy, her daughter. *Our* daughter. They are what I want. Adrianne helped me see that I needed to accept you and Kate together even before Ma's tirade. More importantly, Adrianne deserves a man, not an immature child." Jose puffed out his chest a little. "And that's what I'm going to be. Now that I've finally found what I want, I'm going to do everything in my power to keep it."

Diego tried to absorb everything Jose had just said. He wanted to ask a million questions, about Adrianne and the child and what exactly he'd meant about treating him like a grown-up, but Jose continued before he had the chance.

"It's time you move home, take over the riding school for good and do the happily-ever-after thing. And I'll take care of this stuff here," he finished, gesturing at the desk covered in papers.

"What's happened to you?" Diego asked at last.

Jose gave his brother a wide grin. "When I saw Adrianne again, it was like nothing changed. I still wanted her. I've always wanted her. But she said I was too immature and she couldn't get involved with me, not when there's a kid involved. And then she and I had some serious conversations after, well," he said with a little cough, "that incident in the barn. And this is right, for all of us. So I'm going to straighten up and show her that she can trust me to be the man she deserves. Ma's call just solidified everything a little more for me. So I came to find you."

Diego had never seen his brother look so determined. He didn't doubt that this man could do everything he'd set his mind to.

Diego wanted to take Jose at his word and run back to Kate, but he still couldn't shake the feeling that the universe didn't want him to have her, that his happiness wasn't a good enough reason. "When Hannah fell off that horse, it was a sign that I needed to focus on work, not her and the riding school. I don't belong there."

Jose snorted. "The only thing her injury was a sign of was that Jonas doesn't understand the difference between a practical joke and a death trap."

"Jonas?" Diego said, confused.

"Yeah," Jose shrugged. "Ma told me that he came by with his parents to apologize. Apparently he confessed to loosening the cinch strap while you and Kate were helping other kids. He thought it would be funny."

Diego didn't say anything for a long minute. "It wasn't my fault," he said at last. The last burden of shame and regret evaporated from his shoulders.

"Nope, just a punk kid. Honestly, I don't know why you love the riding school and hate our business," Jose said, patting the desk fondly.

For what seemed like the hundredth time that day, Diego was taken by surprise. "I never said that I hated—" he began, wondering how the conversation had gotten away from him like this.

Jose cut him off with a raised eyebrow and sardonic smile. "You think I don't know you at least that well? Of course you don't want to buy and sell rodeo stock. I've known that since we started this thing."

Diego felt a small flash of anger. "Then why didn't you say anything this whole time?"

"Why didn't *you* say anything?" Jose countered. Then he grew serious again. "I was hoping you'd come around to it eventually. I was worried if I did it without you, we'd drift apart. And silly as it is for a grown man to say, I like talking to you every day."

Diego tried to absorb this on top of everything else. Jose, the guy who tried so hard to care about nothing, suddenly cared about more than Diego had ever expected, including himself.

"Plus," Jose continued, "it was really nice to do almost none of the work."

Diego punched his twin on the arm. Now *that* was the Jose he was used to. Jose rubbed the spot and grinned. "Fair enough. But I've turned over a new leaf. I'll stop being quite so selfish and take over the business so you can go live your dream with Kate, Ma and Pop. Don't know why you'd want to, but—"

Diego hardly heard what Jose was saying. His phone dinged and he grabbed at it, desperately hoping it was Kate telling him it wasn't too late.

The message was from Ma: Kate is buying a ticket back to Chicago.

Diego's heart sank. Was he too late? He jumped up

from the table and grabbed his keys, suddenly very happy that Jose had stolen his drink.

He turned to say something to his brother, he wasn't sure what, but before he could say anything, Jose picked up the bottle and refilled the glass. "You're welcome. Now leave me alone so I can get some work done."

Diego rushed toward the door, tripping over anything and everything in his way. He hardly noticed. The only thing he could think of was getting to Kate before she flew out of his life for good.

As he reached the door, Jose called his name. When Diego turned toward him, Jose tilted the glass toward Diego. "Good luck, brother. Kate deserves a guy like you."

Diego smiled. "You're always going to be my twin brother," he said, realizing it sounded stupid to say only after the words were out.

Jose nodded in a way that showed he understood what Diego meant, then gestured toward the door. "Get going. Love awaits!"

The last thing Diego heard as the door shut behind him was the squeak of his chair as Jose settled in.

Kate leaned against the large ranch house, looking out at the driveway. A small smile twitched at her lips as she watched the truck tear down the driveway. Kate stood and practically skipped down the porch steps as the truck pulled up, Diego in the driver's seat.

Dust flew as he slammed on his breaks, and he was out of the vehicle before it had time to settle. Before

Kate could say a word, his arms were around her and he was kissing her with all his might.

Kate leaned into him, her mind a pleasant blank. It took a long time for them to part. Finally they did, and Kate stared at him.

"You're back," she said with a relieved sigh.

"I know I don't deserve you, but please don't leave," he said, as out of breath as if he'd run ten miles.

"Okay," Kate said, grinning at him.

Diego looked confused. "Okay? That's it?"

"Yeah," Kate told him, wrapping an arm around his neck. "I knew you'd come around sooner or later."

Kate couldn't tell if Diego was more confused or relieved. "Ma said you were leaving," he said, as if she didn't know.

Kate shook her head. "She said I was buying a ticket. Two tickets, actually. But they're for September."

A smile tugged at Diego's lips. "Did she do that on purpose to make me think—"

"Well, *somebody* needed to light a fire under you!" Ma shouted from where she'd been peeking through the cracked door before slamming it closed.

"You said you let your kids make their own mistakes!" Diego shouted at the door, though it was clear by his grin that he wasn't the least bit upset.

The door opened again, and Ma stood there with her hands on her hips. "I didn't say I never nudge you in the right direction if you're being a darn fool," she retorted.

Kate chuckled. "To be fair, it wasn't all her idea. I had to give it one more shot," she said, looking determinedly at Diego. "I think this thing is going to be worth fighting for. Do you?"

In answer, he kissed her so thoroughly it made her toes curl. Then he pressed his forehead against hers, cupping her cheeks with his hands. "I am so sorry, Kate," he said, emphasizing each word. "I was wrong and I hurt you in the process. I love you and I want to be with you. I'll spend the rest of my life trying to make it up to you, if you'll let me. I love you, Kate," he repeated, as if he wanted to hear himself say it.

"So you're not going to try to be honorable anymore?" she asked with a little smile.

"Absolutely not," he said with a shake of his head and a wicked smirk. His voice dropped so Ma, who was still standing in the doorway looking very pleased with herself, wouldn't hear. "In fact, if you're up for it, I'd like to do some very dishonorable things with you."

They kissed again until they were both panting. Kate leaned against him. "So, where are we going in September?" he asked.

"We're going to visit my family. I'd like to get to know my parents and half sibiings as an adult. And I want them to meet my boyfriend," she said, patting his chest.

Diego moved back and held her at arm's length. "You really think I'll be your boyfriend two months from now?" he asked, sounding skeptical.

It was her turn to be confused. "You don't?" she asked.

He shook his head. "Nah. Fiancé, probably. Maybe husband. Or baby daddy or—"

She rolled her eyes at him and they smiled at each other like a couple of fools.

"You never gave up on me, even when I was such an idiot as to think I could live a life without you," he said, shaking his head in amazement.

Kate shrugged. "What can I say? I take after Ma," she said, tilting her head toward the older woman.

Diego laughed a little. "You're not even related to her," he said.

"Future in-law. Close enough," she told him with a smile.

Epilogue

"Are you almost ready?" Kate asked, not taking her eyes from the baby she was carefully settling into the car seat. The child cooed and stuck a fist into his drooling mouth.

Diego sat with their son, sticking yet another bow onto the already covered present. "Just about. Danny thinks we need more bows," he told her with a wink.

"Bow!" the toddler agreed enthusiastically.

Kate laughed, a clear ringing sound that never failed to reach straight to Diego's heart.

Once the bag of bows was completely empty, Danny pronounced the present ready and the family of four piled into the cab of their truck.

"We're a little late," Diego said when the time flashed on the dashboard.

"Oh, well," Kate told him. "Amy will understand. With three kids, I'm amazed they ever make it anywhere at all."

"At least we'll be there before Jose," Diego added.

"I don't know about that," Kate said thoughtfully. "He and Adrianne are usually on the ball."

Diego considered this. "You know, you're right. I'm just so used to his old ways that every once in a while I forget. He's been like a different person since they got together and he became a father."

"It's been six years since that happened," Kate reminded him.

"Feels like yesterday," Diego told his wife with a quick kiss before putting the truck into Reverse.

They drove up to Jack and Amy's house. There were several cars and trucks parked outside, and the front of the house was covered in streamers and balloons. "Looks like Ma has been very busy the last few hours," Kate said, surveying the decor.

On the porch there was a basket of silly hats, glasses and necklaces, something that had become a family tradition over the years. After properly festooning themselves, the family walked through the partially open front door into the surprisingly quiet house.

As they began to make their way through the living room, Jose appeared with a drink in his hand. "You're late, you know," he said with a wide grin.

Diego smiled at his twin brother. "It's good to see you, too. Where is everybody?"

Adrianne walked in and slipped her arm around her husband's waist. "Darcy wanted a bounce house for her birthday, so the party is outside this year. Zach and Carter are teaching their younger cousins how to almost break their necks doing somersaults."

Diego laughed. "So a typical six-year-old's party, huh?"

Jose beckoned and Diego followed with his family. "How's work?" Diego asked as they all trooped outside. "Busy as usual?"

Jose grinned. "I told you buying and selling rodeo stock was a great idea. But no, you wanted to teach kids how to hold reins over and over instead," he said with a shake of his head.

Diego shrugged. Even though Jose had made their business wildly successful since Diego left, he wouldn't have it any other way. Even if it meant he had to take a bit of ribbing from his twin when they got together.

As they wound their way toward the prominent bounce house, a large pink inflatable castle, a young girl ran up to them. "Happy birthday, Darcy!" Diego and Kate said as she gave each of them a quick hug before she ran away again to play.

Diego gave Amy, who had clearly taught her daughter to greet the guests, a thumbs-up. He couldn't believe Darcy was born six years ago. He looked at his wife, who was holding their youngest in her arms. So much had happened since Darcy entered the world.

Ma rushed up to them, a wide smile on her face. "Oh, good, everybody's here. How are you, my dears?"

Diego chuckled. "Nothing much has changed since you left the house three hours ago," he said, earning himself a slap on the arm from his adoptive mother.

"Just because Jose acts his age, you need to be a smart aleck? What did I do to deserve such rascals?" she said, looking up to the sky in supplication.

"I resent that," Jose said, crossing his arms in front of his chest. "I may have matured a little, but I refuse to act my age. And I'm still the biggest smart aleck in the family. I'll defend that title until my dying day," he concluded with a dramatic flourish.

Nobody argued with him.

Ma picked up Danny with a grunt. "My, you've grown since this morning," she said, bouncing him as if she was checking his weight. Soon the two of them were giggling like coconspirators.

Kate and Diego sat with the other adults, who were half watching the insanity of the bounce house while trying to keep up with multiple conversations with their family members.

Diego looked around at his family, everyone talking and laughing, surrounded by the shouts of happy children, and everyone sporting a ridiculous pair of dollar-store glasses.

"What are you thinking about over there?" Kate asked, squeezing his leg with her hand.

Diego looked into her green eyes and smiled wistfully. "I just wish Pop could see all this," he told her.

"You don't think he's looking down at all of us and sporting a grin the size of Texas?" Ma said, not taking her eyes off the grandson in her arms.

Kate grasped his hand. "Pop would be so proud of this whole big family, don't you think?" she said quietly.

Diego nodded. Every McNeal was married, deeply

in love and surrounded by children, all living in Spring Valley, the best little town in Texas. What more was there to say?

Diego kissed his wife and leaned back in his seat, content with the world.

* * * * *